# The Wishing Tree

BARBARA WINKES

ISBN 978-1-7781247-8-5

Created with Atticus

*For D.*

# Chapter One

## STEVIE

W hen Stevie entered Suzy's café to the tune of *My Grown-up Christmas List*, Ana was already seated at a table, cradling the light blue mug in her hand as if to draw warmth from it. Stevie suppressed a sigh before she put what she hoped was an encouraging smile on her face.

She could read her best friend's expression easily, and it told her that Ana's meeting with her parents hadn't gone well. That, on top of having been dumped by her girlfriend, could ruin a person's holidays.

Not that Stevie cared so much about the celebrations, but Ana did, a lot, and that was good enough for her.

"Hey," she said as she joined her at the table. "You're here early."

"Yeah. I couldn't stand being home alone. At least it's warm and everyone is friendly here."

No one could argue with that. At Suzy's, everyone was welcome, and during Christmas time, they went all out. It had become Stevie and Ana's favorite place since they'd been Freshmen, and even now, after graduation, they kept coming back.

Ana got up to hug her, and Stevie squeezed tightly.

"What's going on?"

They both sat down. The music had changed to an upbeat song about the wonders of Christmas, and it couldn't be a more jarring contrast to the tears forming in Ana's eyes. She wiped them away in a hasty gesture when the waitress approached their table.

"A cinnamon chocolate latte, and a pear brioche, please," Stevie told her, making Ana laugh.

"I am so grateful for the things that never change. Black coffee, please, and an oatmeal muffin."

"For someone who likes Christmas so much, you have trouble indulging yourself."

"Yeah, you would know. It might be that lately I don't feel like I deserve it." Stevie opened her mouth to protest, but Ana made a dismissive gesture. "Please, hear me out. I can't help thinking there must be something I did wrong, and I know you're going to tell me in a minute that none of it is my fault. But there must be a way, something I can do."

Stevie had some ideas, none of which she would share with Ana. She had already told her, and meant it, that she could do so much better than Patricia, a woman who had never shown any patience or understanding for Ana's situation.

"What do you have in mind?"

Talking about Ana's parents was another tricky subject. Stevie knew that Ana loved them, and she would never keep her distance, no matter how stubborn they were. Stevie had known them for a long time, and everyone was always polite with each other. That didn't make up for the fact that they had reacted badly when Ana came out to them, and they kept making it worse.

"I can't not spend Christmas with my family."

Ana wiped away another tear, the sight stirring a familiar anger in Stevie. Why did people have to be deliberately cruel, especially when it came to holidays associated with family? She had no patience or understanding for that. She didn't think anyone should.

"Are you sure it's a good idea?" she asked carefully. "You know I'm staying in town. We could always hang out, even watch some Christmas movies if you like. I'll visit my mom after the holidays as always. Wait!" She had an even better idea. "Why don't you join me? You know she wouldn't mind."

In Stevie's house, no one had ever put pressure on anyone to be or act a certain way. She had grown up thinking that much about Christmas was pretense, and a commercial ruse. If you loved each other, there was no need for any of it, though there had been presents for her and her older brother. Sometimes on Christmas Day. Sometimes in the new year. They had learned not to yield to the marketing strategies of shops and churches, and they were happy.

Things were different in Ana's family, and despite the short-comings of her loved ones, she held on to those traditions. Stevie didn't have the heart to tell her otherwise but showing her a celebration that was about love and kindness rather than rituals could be a good idea.

"Thank you, but...I can't. I must make things right with them."

That right there. Ana hadn't done anything wrong, so why would it be up to her to make things right? In Stevie's opinion, Ana's entire family owed her an apology and the best Christmas ever. Instead of pointing that out, she nodded.

"I understand. But you don't have to go right away, do you? We'll have some time to go to the market, maybe skating?"

3

"Sure." Ana's eyes lit up at the suggestion. "I still have a few gifts to buy too. You still do gifts, right?"

"Yes, we do."

"Great. But this is not why I asked you to come." She took a sip of her coffee. "I know you think I should handle things with them differently."

"I'd never tell you what to do." Much as sometimes, she wished she could.

Ana reached out to squeeze her hand.

"Don't worry, I know that. Like I said, I have to do something, and I have an idea. Have you heard of the Wishing Tree in Angel Falls?"

Stevie had, and even the terminology was everything her parents had warned her about. She had dismissed the story quickly. The fact that Ana brought it up in the context of fixing her family relations concerned her. No, alarm was more like it.

"You know that's a myth, right?"

Ana shrugged. "What about Christmas isn't?"

She had a point, Stevie couldn't deny it. Still.

"You're not serious. You want to go to Angel Falls and put a piece of paper on that tree?"

"That's how it works, I think. Yes, I want to do that. And Stevie, I want you to go with me."

Her jaw dropped.

"What?"

"Don't look so surprised." Ana laughed before her expression turned somber again. "I'd be too embarrassed to ask anyone else, with the mess I've made of my life—"

"You haven't. No, Ana—"

"I need this. It's my last resort. I can't think of anything else. Please?"

"You'll be so disappointed if it doesn't work out. And besides, I don't believe in any of it. Isn't that, I don't know, bad luck?"

"You could never bring me bad luck," Ana declared. "I have to do this, and you have to come with me. It will be fun! A road trip before Christmas. I know you like those. And you said you have time."

It occurred to Stevie that Ana had already given this a lot of thought. What was she to do? She was single, and her mother didn't expect her before December 29th. Besides, Ana needed someone beside her who wouldn't say *told you so* when her wish didn't come true, and her parents didn't magically come to their senses on Christmas Eve.

Did she ever really have a choice?

Ana gave her a knowing smile. "Say yes. You know it's going to be awesome. Since you'll be with me, you could make another wish for me, and maybe Pat will return my calls."

"Don't push it," Stevie warned. "All right. I'll come with you, we do what people do there, and then we come back home."

"Great. I've already booked us a room for the long weekend. Don't worry, it's all paid."

Money was the last thing Stevie was worried about, but that, too, she kept to herself.

"Merry Christmas, Stevie. You're the best."

"Merry Christmas."

She was a good friend, no doubt about it. And she was going to be in so much trouble.

·♥·♥·♥·♥·♥·

Angel Falls was a quaint little town a little over three hours away, and Stevie could have done without ever seeing it. That was no longer an option.

The next couple of days, she was busy wrapping up things at work. Stevie hadn't planned on taking a two-week vacation, but she had failed to take those days earlier in the year, and if she didn't do it now, she'd lose them. She loved her job as a pediatric nurse, had worked during the holidays for as long as she'd been employed with the city hospital. It worked well for her since she rarely saw her mother and brother on Christmas Day.

This year, it wasn't such bad timing. She would take Ana to Angel Falls and see her mother and Evan after Christmas. After their father's death, they held on to some traditions. No obligatory tree, specific food, or carols though.

On the way home, she brought take-out from the Chinese place in her neighborhood, another restaurant she and Ana had discovered together and loved. Patricia hadn't loved it, but Stevie had decided that the woman didn't appreciate anything good.

Patricia was in the past, and Ana would get over her eventually. Stevie frowned at the images on her phone. If her parents didn't come around, it was questionable if Ana could get over it, and Stevie doubted that the Wishing Tree would do the trick.

Something more had to happen. Maybe she was the one who had to make it happen. She abandoned her train of thought, aware that she was getting far ahead of herself.

There was something she could do though, make sure Ana had a few nice days to soften the blow of what was no doubt waiting for her at home.

Stevie could do that, couldn't she?

The pictures she had found of Angel Falls online, from the town's official website, bloggers and tourists, looked almost unreal, like something out of a Christmas movie. Sure, she liked to go skating in the winter, enjoy a mug of mulled wine or two, but this? It looked like every single building in the small town was decorated to the hilt. Besides boasting the Wishing Tree that ten-thousands of visitors flocked to every year, the town celebrated an annual tree lighting and offered various activities for children and adults.

They had a *Christmas Inn*.

Stevie shook her head at the excess of it all, and then she realized that this was the place Ana had booked for them. It was likely expensive. There had to be a more reasonable option in or around town? After all, they weren't going to stay long, just hang Ana's wish on the tree, explore the town a bit, and go home?

There couldn't be that much to explore anyway.

"What did I say yes to?" she said out loud and winced when it felt like the words echoed in the room around her. She and Ana had been roommates at some point, then after graduation they had both moved into their respective apartments to be close to work. Stevie missed those days. She came close to moving in with her boyfriend last summer, but out of the blue he had decided he was destined for bigger and better things, which meant he wasn't ready for any commitment.

Stevie didn't have such a hard time letting him go, and it was during long conversations with Ana over wine or tea, depending on the time of day, that she learned she might not be ready either.

She had gone out with a few people since then, mostly first dates that didn't lead anywhere. Stevie had considered using her unexpectedly long vacation to try out a dating app or go the old-fashioned route, but now she had plans.

Funny how they made her feel better because she'd spend time with Ana, even though the circumstances weren't that great.

They would get through this, together, as always. Ana would find someone who wasn't going to dictate the pace of her coming out for her.

Stevie would find someone she wanted to be with all of the time.

It could happen at Christmas.

Or at any time.

# Chapter Two

## ANA

Ana knew it wasn't the best idea, but she hadn't lied to Stevie: It was the only idea she had left. And she wasn't going to give up without trying everything she could. She would give Stevie credit for not rolling her eyes and only half-heartedly trying to stop her.

What Ana needed was nothing short of a miracle. If she was honest, she was aware of the odds, and even at Christmas, they weren't in her favor.

Especially at Christmas. Maybe she was petty, but on a holiday that was all about love, shouldn't her parents come around? Shouldn't they see that she still was the same person?

They wanted her to deny who she was, who she still was even after Patricia had left her, unwilling to wait for Ana to claim her space in the world and in the community they shared.

Fortunately, she shared that same community with Stevie, something she hadn't even been aware of until recent years. It wasn't that Stevie didn't trust her. In fact, in their first year in college, Ana had been the first person Stevie had come out to as bi—even before her open-minded, unconditionally loving parents, before any other friend or family member.

Because they knew they could share everything. It didn't matter that Ana came from a conservative family, or that Stevie's tended to ignore holidays for the most part. They trusted each other, had for a long time, and this was why Stevie was the only one she could ask to go on that desperate trip—adventure—with her.

Not long ago, Ana had thrived on Christmas cheer, and she had dreamed of visiting a town like Angel Falls. See the lights, sample all the good food and drinks a place like this undoubtedly had to offer. Attend a service in the magnificent church, marvel at the Christmas decorations.

And the Wishing Tree.

Her hopes and dreams might be in a rather disastrous state, but she had this one last chance to turn it all around. If it didn't happen, at least she wouldn't be alone.

Standing on the curb with her backpack and suitcase, Ana shuddered at the thought that all of this might be in vain. Where would she go from there? What would future Christmases be like, if her loved ones didn't want her there?

Lonely, she thought, then she remembered Stevie's offer. She might be brokenhearted for many reasons, but Stevie was the one constant in her life, without fail.

If they couldn't make miracles happen, they would at least have all the fun they could in Angel Falls. Ana was determined. She would put that wish on the famous Wishing Tree, and trust in whatever Higher Power was supposed to be behind it.

They would have a few days of uninterrupted, untainted Christmas magic, and perhaps she could convert Stevie as well?

The thought made her smile. Probably not, but the fact that she'd be there meant everything to Ana.

·♥·♥·♥·♥·♥·

Stevie arrived at 9:00 a.m. sharp, the time they had agreed on, but Ana had left her apartment so early—again—that she could barely feel her fingers in the thin gloves.

She sighed in relief when she got into the car. It was toasty in here, the seat warmer a gift from heaven.

"You could have stayed inside," Stevie chided gently. "Did you think that I was going to leave without you?"

"That could have happened. I know you can't wait to get to Angel Falls," Ana said with a straight face, and they both burst out laughing.

"Right. Okay. Breakfast first?"

"You got it."

Her mother had instilled in her not to leave the house without breakfast, but Ana didn't want to think of her, or her advice now.

Whatever happened after the trip, she would at least make one dream come true.

But yes, breakfast first.

·♥·♥·♥·♥·♥·

They stopped at the first diner out of town, a charming place hidden from the road all decorated for Christmas. Ana couldn't help it, the lights and music everywhere she went made her hopeful that her life could someday be less chaotic, less scary.

She caught the smile on Stevie's face, the hint of amusement, and she rolled her eyes at her. Stevie laughed, but she made no attempt at denying the charge. Thank God for a friend like Stevie. Yes, Ana knew that she wasn't into any of this. Yet, she was here, on her way to Christmas Central with Ana, indulging every staple of the holiday along the way.

Well, it wasn't like she didn't get anything out of it.

The diner offered a holiday special brunch, and given the effort she was making, Ana, too, felt like she deserved a little indulgence.

They sat in a booth by the window, a friendly server arriving with coffee right away.

"The special for both of you?"

"Yes, please, thank you."

"How did he know?" Stevie asked, confused, when he had left.

"I don't know, maybe the way your face lit up when you saw the sign, gave him a hint?"

"You're incorrigible. You're having it too."

"Yes. I get the feeling we need to brace ourselves. For many things."

Stevie's features softened, understanding in her expression. Of course, she understood, knew Ana better than anyone.

She wasn't naïve. She knew that her parents and siblings had a long way to go, and that so far, they hadn't shown much interest in taking even small steps. But she believed they were able to. They had loved her once, and they could do so again.

Meanwhile, she would hopefully find the courage for all the steps *she* needed to take. She cast a glance outside the window where a few snowflakes were dancing in the wind. As a child she had always wished for snow on the ground. Sometimes it happened, sometimes it didn't, but she was never not excited for the holidays, the time spent with her extended family, the brightness of it all.

But light wasn't just pretty. It also exposed.

She turned back to Stevie who was checking the weather forecast on her phone but looking up as if she sensed Ana's gaze on her.

"It will be fine. They say there'll be a storm on Christmas Day, but we'll be long home by then."

"Yeah. Look, Stevie...I wanted to say I'm so grateful you're doing this with me."

"Are you kidding? I wouldn't miss it for the world." One look from Ana was enough to make her clarify. "Okay, I could do without the over-the-top holiday cheer, but I get to spend more time with you. That is a good reason."

Before the moment could get any more emotional, the server returned with their plates, and no one could get sentimental in the face of this abundance, eggs, toast, fruit, waffles with cranberry-orange cream. They had gone with the non-alcoholic "mimosa," given that they'd both drive.

Stevie raised her glass.

"To us doing everything we put our minds to, and generally being awesome."

"To us," Ana echoed, even though she would have liked to toast to something more specific regarding their endeavor—to miracles or wishes coming true.

It was still early.

She was going to enjoy every moment of it.

When they were ready to leave, Stevie suggested a quick stop at the restroom.

"I'll be fine."

"Are you sure? We said we wanted to make it at least halfway there before another coffee?"

"It's all right," Ana insisted. "I'm good. You go."

Stevie gave her a doubtful look, but she shrugged and headed for the restroom, while Ana lingered near the entrance.

When Stevie returned, she tried once more. "Last chance."

"I told you, I'm good."

"Let's go then," Stevie relented and held the door open for Ana on their way out.

A few snowflakes caught in their hair before they made it back to the car. Ana cast a sideways glance at her friend, snow melting in her strawberry blonde hair, her cheeks pink with the cold.

A stray thought sprang to mind, and she wondered why Stevie hadn't dated anyone in months.

To her, she had always been gorgeous. Of course, Stevie loved her job, and she rarely made time even when she was dating someone. More than once, the other person had taken offense.

Ana understood dedication. She was happy working as a kindergarten teacher, even though she knew her parents would have preferred her to teach at the university, get tenure.

She understood Stevie's dedication. That made it even more special to her that Stevie had dropped everything and come to Angel Falls with her, simply because Ana had asked.

She leaned back in her seat with a smile, then she started playing with the radio and found a Christmas channel.

Perfect.

She started singing along to *Jingle Bell Rock*, stealing glances at Stevie who could barely keep the smile off her face.

"Come on. You know you want to."

"I don't want to," Stevie denied, but the corners of her mouth twitched.

Ana kept singing, and two songs and less than fifteen minutes later, Stevie joined in. They made good headway, while the snowfall intensified some, but not enough to worry.

They also had to find another diner, because Ana needed to pee. She bought a latte for Stevie as an apology, and another one for herself, and it was clear to both of them that this trip would last a little longer than the expected three hours.

# Chapter Three

## STEVIE

A na had offered to drive, but Stevie had declined so far. She liked having something to focus on—like Ana's smile when she was engaged in anything Christmas related, like food, like driving. It kept her nerves at bay. She was enjoying herself, no doubt about it.

Being around her best friend always put her at ease, and they were having fun...That didn't mean this undertaking didn't have tricky parts.

Stevie had a plan B and a plan C, so far, and she hoped she wouldn't have to go down the alphabet to avoid a catastrophe for Christmas.

They would be home before the day, but she had brought Ana's gifts just in case. Angel Falls, with that imposing tree, and the Christmas Inn, might be a great location to celebrate early.

It might become necessary if plan B failed. Stevie would have preferred to make the shaking up of traditions optional. She had yet to see how her scheming would turn out, emails not yet sent, a call or two she planned to make while Ana was distracted.

Stevie would have to be careful, especially when she was still so mad. Ana worked as hard at her job as she did at regaining her family's love. And why would a decent person withhold love from their daughter or sibling anyway, from someone as sweet and kind as Ana?

Stevie had some explanations, but it wasn't up to her to confront anyone with them. That, she knew, would only make things worse. Above all, she wasn't willing to risk their friendship.

She couldn't stand by and let Ana's hopes go up in flames either. If there was a way that she could help make her wish come true, Stevie wouldn't hesitate.

*I know I've been quite cavalier about Christmas Magic, but if you exist, I could use some help.* Right. She wasn't even sure who she was talking to.

"What are you smiling at?" Ana wanted to know. Earlier, the wind had tousled her dark curls, but somehow, she still, always, looked amazing. She had so much going for her. If her family, and pathetic Patricia couldn't see that, it was their loss.

Where did that come from? Stevie had tried to be a good friend, not petty, during Ana's break-up with Patricia. She should try harder because this wouldn't help anyone.

"Just...this," she finally answered the question. "We're trying to evoke Christmas Magic. I'm really, really far out of my depth here."

"It's fine. You'll see, there's nothing much you have to do other than to be present and enjoy it. The way it was when we were kids."

"You know what Christmas was like when Evan and I were kids."

"You had love. Shared meals, gifts on the 15$^{th}$ or 29$^{th}$, or maybe in February, I know. Just because your parents didn't believe in the commercial side of the holiday, it doesn't mean they didn't have the spirit of Christmas or didn't know what it's all about."

"I get you, Linus. Okay, last chance. If we go past the next exit, we'll drive all the way there. You're good?"

Ana, for all her qualities, didn't have the best poker face.

"All right, one more stop, then we'll go all the way to Angel Falls."

Truth be told, Stevie was a bit excited about it too, even though she had no particular wish on her mind.

Well, she did wish she could talk to her dad one more time, but that wasn't possible. Other than that, she had everything in her life she could wish for, didn't she?

♥ · ♥ · ♥ · ♥ · ♥ ·

*Welcome to Angel Falls.* Stevie couldn't help the nagging concern when they made it past the sign and into a winter wonderland. The website hadn't promised too much: Every house in this town that they drove past was joyfully decorated. She could see the church's steeple in the distance.

"The inn is this way," Ana provided, and Stevie took the turn, the desire to stall occupying her mind.

This was supposed to be a time-out, a moment for Ana to take a breath before she spent the holidays with her stubborn family...but what if it wasn't?

Stevie's research hadn't produced much other than stories woven around the famous Wishing Tree. There wasn't much else, nothing to tell her how welcome they would really be in the small town.

What if the people were like Ana's parents? They would ruin everything for her, and Stevie would feel guilty for not having done her homework. She felt a little guilty in advance already, hoping this hadn't been a big mistake.

At least Ana had booked a room with two queen beds, so no one would assume anything, right?

Who was she kidding?

On their first day of college, classmates had thought they were together, and it had taken them both a good amount of dating other people to dispel the rumor. Yet it never seemed completely gone.

*You are spending so much time together!*

Yeah, so?

The point was, she couldn't use any complications. There weren't enough letters in the alphabet if she had to come up with plans, in case the residents of Angel Falls weren't all that nice.

Stevie hoped for the best.

They drove up to the inn that indeed looked like something straight out of a movie: a wreath adorning every window, a decorated tree on the front lawn, and lights strung around the banister of the wraparound porch, and the roof. Stevie could only imagine what the inside looked like.

"How about we check in and then we find someplace to eat? There were a few restaurants on the way."

"How are you hungry again?"

"Hey. That last coffee and donut was a long time ago."

She parked the car and for a few moments, she watched Ana take in the surroundings in awe. So many lights. Ana's profile looked almost angelic in them.

Stevie tore her gaze away, reminding herself that she was on a mission. No distractions.

"Let's go?"

When Ana hesitated, maybe having some of the same worries she'd contemplated earlier, Stevie took her hand and squeezed it gently.

"It will be fine. I promise."

Ana gave her a grateful smile, and they exited the car, got their suitcases out and headed to the front door. The moment they walked inside, they were greeted by music—of course—and more lights. A woman in her sixties wearing a red sweater with a smiling penguin on it was behind the counter. A Christmas centerpiece sat on said counter, complete with a battery-operated candle.

Next to it was a plate with delicious looking cookies. For guests, she hoped.

"Are you Stevie and Ana?" the woman asked, getting up. "Welcome to the Christmas Inn. We hope you'll have a magic experience. I'm Josephine. Jo."

"Hi, Jo. I booked a room online."

"Yes, I have it here." The woman beamed as she handed Ana the key. "Breakfast is served in the room over there, 7:00 a.m. until noon. Not all of us are early risers, right? The elevator is right behind you, but if you ask me, taking the stairs is worth it. Your room is on the second floor."

"Thank you so much! And sure, we'll take the stairs."

Stevie gave her a quizzical look, but she didn't argue. If taking the stairs made Ana happy, that's what they would do.

"Don't forget this."

Jo handed the plate with the delicious looking cookies, stars, hearts and bells, to them.

"Thank you." Stevie took one, and the woman shook her head. "No, they're all for you. Someone will get you your welcome hot chocolate in a few minutes."

"Our welcome...That's amazing."

"That's why we don't take the elevator." Ana laughed, sounding happy. So far so good.

"Thanks." Stevie took the plate, and they walked over to the impressive wooden staircase leading up to the other floors.

Jo hadn't promised too much. On the way they could see the surrounding landscape through the windows, a beautiful view. All the rooms had old-fashioned door locks to be opened with an actual key.

"I think I checked 'view of the town,'" Ana mumbled as she slid the key into her pocket and stepped aside for Stevie to go in first.

She did and stopped so abruptly that a second later they nearly collided.

"What are you doing...oh." Ana had seen it too. She shrugged. "It's definitely not what I checked, but who cares? It's not like it'll be the first time we share a bed."

No, it wouldn't be. Stevie couldn't quite explain why this time felt different. Maybe it was because they were making the whole trip for the small chance that Ana's family would come around and accept her for who she was, a woman who loved women.

Easy. It should be.

Somehow, this arrangement put a spotlight on everything that might or might not go wrong, or so it felt to Stevie. She wasn't sure anymore. She was tired and hungry—yes, again—and the early dusk didn't help.

"No, it's not," she agreed, turning around to see Jo standing in the doorway, smiling brightly as she held a tray with two mugs.

"Yes, it's me again, everyone downstairs was busy. I'll leave you two alone now but come find me downstairs if you need recommendations for dinner."

Had she overheard their conversation? She didn't seem to care. Stevie breathed a little easier, her smile genuine when she said, "Thank you. We appreciate it."

First impression of Angel Falls, not that bad. At least they wouldn't miss out when it came to food and drink. She put the plate of cookies on the nightstand and took off her boots, before she sat on the bed. Even the foot of it was decorated, and two stockings hung above a small fireplace.

"Is this place for real?" she wondered out loud, and Ana, instead of an answer, hugged her tightly.

"Thank you! Now, let's try those cookies. I know you want to."

Stevie didn't disagree.

# Chapter Four

## ANA

She was stalling. Stevie could probably tell and bless her for not calling Ana out on it. Yes, initially she had intended to go to the Wishing Tree the moment they arrived, for this to be their first activity. Everything else would magically fall into place after that.

Now that they were here in the fabled town, she wasn't so sure anymore.

How long did one have to wait anyway for their wishes to come true? A few days? A month? It would be too late for this Christmas then.

So they sat on the bed—did she imagine that, or had Stevie been the tiniest bit flustered when it turned out they got a room with only one bed?—and shared Jo's delicious cookies and hot chocolate. Sure, Ana could have told Jo that this wasn't the room she'd asked for, but she imagined that the place would be fully booked around this time of year, and she had no intention of going anywhere else.

It wasn't a big deal, was it? They'd been sharing rooms (and tents) on field trips, vacations and various sleepovers, sometimes with others, sometimes just the two of them.

Besides, she had other things to worry about. That tree. What if real magic existed? What if it didn't?

When Ana first heard about the story, something about it called to her, something that told her there was something important for her here. And nothing was more important than family, wasn't it?

"Since we don't have to go to dinner right away, how about we look at some fun things to do around here?"

"You mean like wreath making and snowman building contests?" Stevie quipped, and Ana threw a pillow at her. It might be juvenile, but Stevie bursting into laughter was worth it. There was nothing awkward between them, never had been, and she needed it to stay that way if she wanted to make it through the holidays and beyond.

"You're funny. I checked it out before, and they have a really nice ice rink, a Christmas market, and perhaps we could go see the choir?"

Much as she tried, she couldn't cover up that little hopeful rise of her voice. To be honest, Ana didn't go to church often enough to make it count, at least not in her family's view. But she had always loved Christmas concerts and services, and here, they were at the heart of the celebration.

"Yeah, we can check it out," Stevie agreed. "If the schedule doesn't work, we could just visit the church. They have some cool stained-glass windows."

"I saw that too," Ana said, relieved. "Okay. I'd also like to check out the boutiques along main street, get a few last-minute gifts."

"You bought enough gifts for the next five Christmases when we last went shopping."

She might be offended if this came from anyone else, but Stevie's friendly teasing, Ana could handle.

"Right, Ms. Grinch, and there's always room for more."

"There's also bankruptcy."

"I'll have you know I'm far from it."

"Okay. When will be the big moment?"

With the question, Stevie's tone had gone soft, and a bit anxious.

"I don't know, tomorrow afternoon maybe. Or the day after tomorrow." Ana felt the need to elaborate. "Jo could probably tell us too, but from what I gathered, there's some sort of protocol. You buy a kit. There's a piece of paper with an envelope, and you write your wish on the paper and put it inside. The envelope goes into a glass ball, and you hang it on the tree."

"Nothing is free, even at Christmas," Stevie mused.

"The money goes to food banks and women's shelters. And Planned Parenthood."

"Okay, I'm shutting up now. How about we walk around a bit, get a feel for the place, and afterwards, we go somewhere for dinner? Tomorrow we'll figure out this wishing business, get your kit, and you can put your wish on the tree whenever you're ready."

That sounded like a sensible plan of action, not that she was surprised Stevie had one. Ana had...a wish, and she had booked them the wrong hotel room. Anyway.

"That sounds great. Are you sure you don't want me to pay for gas?"

"Yes, I'm sure. You're already paying for the room, and, really, it's no big deal. So, you want to head out?"

"In a few, yes. I just want to change first."

Stevie's eyes widened when Ana took the dress out of her suitcase.

"You're going to freeze," she said, predictably.

"It's around zero, and I have stockings. I'll be fine."

"If you say so."

"I do say so," Ana said and went into the bathroom, clothes on her arm. She was a pro at wishful thinking, wasn't she? Small things and big things. She had wished that Stevie would come to Angel Falls with her, and that the first person they'd meet would be kind.

So far so good.

·♥·♥·♥·♥·♥·

"Hi Jo," she said when they walked up to the counter. Ana was momentarily distracted by the way Stevie's black plants hugged her figure, her legs appearing even longer in the black ankle boots. The cream-colored sweater created a perfect contrast, and her hair, now free from the ponytail, came down to her shoulders in waves.

Ana cleared her throat. "You said earlier you could give us some suggestions for dinner?"

"Of course. Give me just a second."

Jo was in the process of checking in other guests. Two men in their thirties had a girl of about six years old with them, and behind them, a man and a woman in their fifties waited, chatting with the other couple, and gushing over the girl.

It took a little more than a second, but Jo headed over to them with a cheery smile and handed them three leaflets.

"It all depends on what you're in the mood for. I have a diner for you, a pizzeria, and Asian Fusion. The latter is a bit fancier, but I see you're dressed for it. They are all within walking distance. You take the path you came on earlier, and it shouldn't take you longer than ten minutes to get to Main Street. From there, you can't miss any of them."

26

"Sounds easy enough," Stevie agreed. "Thank you again. We might try all of them while we're here."

"You do that. They are all wonderful in their own way."

They stepped outside, and to Ana's relief the temperature felt manageable.

She linked an arm through Stevie's, and they followed Jo's directions to the town's Main Street.

"Isn't it magical?" Ana whispered. She couldn't help it, and she thought that Stevie wasn't completely immune to the effect of sparkling lights everywhere they looked, and the delicious scents from the Christmas market. The latter would have to wait, or they would never get dinner.

They walked along decorated businesses and private residences, a bookstore, a café, the diner Jo had mentioned, and a couple of clothing stores that had all their winter accessories on display, hats, scarves, and gloves. A quaint display decorated the window of a grocery store, figurines skating on a frozen lake.

There, at the end of the street, on the marketplace with the cobblestone, stood the famous tree, already holding a multitude of wishes. Next to it stood a booth that was now closed, where the hopeful could buy their wishing kits from 6:00 a.m. to 6:00 p.m. They had missed it by only a little over an hour, but Ana couldn't hold back a sigh of relief. She wasn't ready.

She wasn't sure what she was doing, at all, if she had to find the perfect words to make her wish come true, or if there was a limit as to how many wishes the tree granted every year. What if they were already too late?

But no, it said on the sign that the booth was open until Christmas Eve.

They still had time.

She shivered, and Stevie moved closer to her immediately. She didn't say I told you so, and besides, Ana wasn't cold, just...scared. Having her closest friend by her side made all the difference though.

"Those cookies were delicious, but I think I'm hungry now," she said.

"Me too. We'll come back tomorrow then. What are you in the mood for?"

"They all sounded good, but how about the fancy one? Jo seemed to think they'd let us in."

"All right. *The Lotus Garden* it is."

⋅♥⋅♥⋅♥⋅♥⋅♥⋅

They turned away from the tree and headed back to the restaurant where a friendly hostess greeted them.

"I'm sorry we are full, but if you are willing to wait for ten, fifteen minutes at the bar, I'll have a table for you, and a welcome drink on the house."

Ana shared a look with Stevie, and they almost spoke in unison.

"That would be great. "

"Thank you, that's great!"

The hostess smiled knowingly and directed them to the bar. Less than a couple of minutes later, they had a drink in front of them, and the server described the ingredients.

Ana and Stevie clinked their glasses together, and she finally felt the stress of the past few months release her. She was in a town that was all about Christmas, in a beautiful restaurant, about to have dinner with her best friend in the world. What was the worst that could happen?

Ana took another sip and set the delicious concoction back on the bar.

"Everyone is really nice here, don't you think?"

"We've only met two people so far, but...yes."

She noticed that Stevie seemed a bit distracted. "Is everything okay?"

That got her Stevie's full attention and one of her amazing smiles. "Absolutely. Everything is going according to plan so far, isn't it?"

"Yes. I'm a bit nervous," she admitted and reached for her glass again. "What if I don't find the right words?"

"Something tells me it's not about making it perfect, though I know you will."

The warmth that filled her might have to do with the alcohol. It might have been for another reason, but that moment, the hostess returned to inform them that their table was ready now.

Ana didn't question the sensation. She'd been antsy and worried for months now, and right now, right here, she felt good. She wanted to hold on to that as long as possible.

They had a scrumptious meal of Vietnamese rolls, Thai chicken and Japanese cheesecake that came with a pretty swirl of strawberry coulis.

In between courses, they caught each other up on things that had happened this year other than the drama with Patricia and her parents. Stevie told her about getting together with colleagues to create a surprise for one of their co-workers which was almost ruined when the person with the cake arrived later than the one whose birthday it was. She also shared some happy stories about children's reactions when they got a visit from the hospital's service dog.

She was good at telling stories too, no surprise there since Stevie constantly had her nose in a book since the moment Ana had met her. In fact, it was Stevie who had inspired her love for reading when she introduced her to the world of sapphic fiction, at a time when Ana thought she'd never have the time or inclination to read much.

Currently, she made Ana laugh so hard her stomach ached, or perhaps it was from too much good food and drink. Could you really have too much of a good thing, of happiness?

As they were leaving, a group of six came in, among them a woman with light purple hair that caught Ana's eye. The woman caught her watching and gave her an amused smile, making her blush and look away.

She knew what her parents would have to say about the hairdo.

She found it pretty.

People had often told her she needed to form her own opinions, distance herself from her family's shortsightedness. It wasn't that easy.

Stevie had never made her choose like Patricia had, even though Ana knew she disapproved of the way they had all reacted to her coming out.

Maybe it was for the best that the latter didn't answer her calls. Ana realized that this might have been the longest she had gone without thinking about her, or what she could have done to make her stay since their break-up.

That brought her back to her biggest, most important wish.

Tomorrow would be the day.

# Chapter Five

## STEVIE

S tevie still hadn't sent those emails, but in her defense, she hadn't had much of an opportunity, much less to sneak away for a phone call. Like Ana she was obsessing on choosing her words wisely. The last thing she wanted was to make things worse.

When the moment came, she wouldn't have much time.

Those musings kept her awake long after Ana had fallen asleep.

People put so much pressure on themselves getting everything right for the holidays, including the perfect family get-together. Stevie could understand why her parents had been leery of that, and why many other people were.

On the other hand, Angel Falls had a surprisingly calming effect she found hard to ignore. It might have to do with the woman snoring softly by her side, because Ana and Christmas were so closely associated. The true meaning of it anyway, the kindness, the generosity.

She appreciated that the people here seemed genuine as well, at least the ones they had run into. The Wishing Tree, of course, was a tourist attraction, plain and simple, and the business owners benefited from it.

It was intriguing to say the least.

Tomorrow, they would go back to get the kit, and then Stevie would be running out of time. Ana had been brave to come out to her parents, even bring Patricia over a couple of times—which had clearly not been enough for Patricia.

Regardless, Stevie had to be brave too. And she would be, aware of what was on the line.

She lay back, startled when Ana made a sound in her sleep and turned around, her hand touching Stevie's side.

Stevie knew from experience that Ana never stayed on her side, but at least she wasn't hogging the covers yet.

What if she bought a kit too? Was there even anything she desired that was worth putting on a piece of paper? She had a job she enjoyed doing, a loving family, at least what was left of it, her group of friends...and she had Ana. Wouldn't it be ungrateful to ask for anything else?

Maybe, Stevie admitted, there was something she missed. Not Luke, or any of the people she had gone out with once or twice after they broke up. None of them were right for her, she knew, and yet she missed the togetherness, being with someone.

That wasn't reason enough to go with just anyone or write it out on a piece of paper. She'd be fine. She should get a pet, or, better yet, start with a plant. If she managed to keep it alive, she could go from there.

Stevie pulled the covers up higher and turned around again, only to flinch again when Ana snuggled up against her back, laying an arm around her waist.

Yes, she was a cuddler too, not that she would remember anything the next morning.

Somehow, Stevie didn't mind.

·♥·♥·♥·♥·♥·

She snuck out of bed a few minutes before seven, had showered and dressed by the time Ana started stirring. Stevie knew Ana was stalling, but maybe she was stalling too. She had those emails ready to go, but she was still debating with herself whether it was better to go all in first, make that call, try her best? Plan C? D?

She could have done any of it while Ana was asleep, but now it was too late. Or maybe not, because she knew Ana would spend quite a bit of time in the bathroom. Too close though.

Ana yawned and got out of bed, looking adorable in her PJs sporting happy snow people. The sight made Stevie happy too.

"You're up already...and dressed."

"And hungry," Stevie added. "You better get going."

"You're always hungry, but you do have a point. I am too. All right." Ana raked a hand through her disheveled hair that looked soft and inviting...

Whoa, what was that?

Stevie could feel her cheeks heat, but Ana had already turned her back to her, rummaging in the drawer of the dresser they were sharing to take out a set of dark blue lingerie.

Stevie busied herself looking at her phone until she had disappeared into the bathroom.

No, seriously, what was that? She had to install that dating app ASAP. Stevie found it in her browsing history and clicked the rainbow heart. She quickly filled in some of the basic information for her profile and added a selfie she wasn't too embarrassed about. No, wait, that was a picture Ana had taken. Stevie wasn't a fan of having her picture taken, one of the reasons why she had stalled on the dating app, but Ana had a talent. When she was finishing up the first step, a text from her mother came in.

*-How are you doing?*

That was a little odd, out of the blue.

*-Good. You?*

*-Fine. You're still coming on the 29^{th}? Have you booked your flight yet?*

Oh, shoot. She had been so busy being mad at Ana's parents and preparing for this trip, that she'd completely forgotten about it.

*-I'll do it today. Sorry, there's been a lot going on. I'll tell you later.*

Her mother, too, was dismayed with the reaction of Ana's family. More like disgusted. Stevie sighed. She was walking on thin ice, or at least she would be if she went through with her plan. A or B.

*-How about you come on the 26^{th}? Evan will be here early too, with his girlfriend. You could bring someone.*

*-I could book an earlier flight. But I'll just bring myself. Still single.*

*-That's fine too. We love you, and you're more than enough.*

This wasn't the first time she'd told Stevie that, it was just the way her family had always talked, and they meant it too...but at this moment, it made her tear up. Everyone should have someone in their lives who loved them unconditionally, family, a significant other...a friend. That was who she was trying to be, but was she doing it right?

Only time could tell.

*-Thank you, Mom. I'll text you the details when I know them.*

She put her phone in her pocket only to see Ana standing in front of her, looking concerned.

"What's going on? Are you okay? Bad news?"

"No, just the opposite." Stevie cleared her throat and got to her feet. "I might go to see my mom sooner. Evan wants to introduce his girlfriend."

"That's nice."

"It is." Too late, it occurred to her that Ana might not want to hear about her happy family at this moment. "Ready?"

"Oh yes." Ana startled her by hugging her, and then Stevie knew without a doubt that her hair was soft, because it tickled her cheek. Her mind wandered back to the previous night, the way they had slept cuddled up together. And as predicted, Ana didn't remember anything.

She was overdue to find herself a few dates. Soon.

·♥·♥·♥·♥·♥·

They had a leisurely breakfast in the dining room, where Jo introduced them to the server, a woman in her twenties who was equally as friendly.

Stevie wasn't ready yet to let her guard down completely. Small towns with longstanding traditions, it could be tricky. Some of her friends had basically fled them, from family situations like Ana's, from neighbors whose noses were always in everybody's business.

A town like in the movies didn't exist, so with all the glitter and gold and friendliness of Angel Falls, there had to be a catch somewhere, right?

Stevie was the cynical one—she could handle it. For Ana's sake, she hoped that they would leave before they had a chance to find it. In terms of disillusionment, she'd had her share this year.

After breakfast, they wandered around town, drifting in and out of the various shops and boutiques. Beautiful wooden sculptures, candles of every shape and scent. The café offered multiple Christmas treats, and another store offered jams and honey.

"You'll definitely find some nice gifts here," Stevie offered.

"Yes. I thought we could do that later in the afternoon? I think I want to get one of those kits before they're out."

Secretly, Stevie doubted it would make any difference whatsoever, but she just nodded and smiled.

"Sure."

This time, the booth was open, and there was a small line of about a dozen people.

To distract herself, Stevie observed the group, noticing that they looked to be of all ages and backgrounds. They had one thing in common: The excitement and joy on their faces.

For a Christmas tradition? For a hoax? It was hard to tell, but all of a sudden, she wished it was New Year's Eve, and Ana's family had come to their senses, so they could celebrate somewhere with friends.

So much could go wrong at this point.

She would try to be there and listen, as always, the way Ana had done it for her for many years.

In the pocket of her coat, she crossed her gloved fingers when they had reached the booth, and Ana chose a kit with a light blue square of paper and envelope, and the iconic clear ornament.

"There's not a lot of space to write on," Ana mused when they were walking away from the newly formed queue.

"I guess that means you have to be short and specific."

"Look at you, expert on wish-making."

Ana's gentle teasing didn't bother her, or the price she'd paid for the items. It was for a good cause after all. Stevie had picked up leaflets from the charities the proceeds would go to this year. Reading over one, from a shelter for unhoused persons, she was happy to see LGBTQ+ youth welcome. At the same time, the context made her shiver, with both the cold, and well, anger.

Ana was lucky that she didn't depend on her parents anymore, not that she would have ever found herself on the street. Stevie certainly didn't trust Ana's family to make the right decision, but her mother, and her father who was still alive when they met in high school, would have never let that happen.

Stevie would have never let it happen. She shook herself out of creating past worst-case scenarios and turned back to the booth.

"Are you going to make a wish too?" Ana asked, sounding much too excited at the prospect. Stevie loved her passion but leaving her deepest hopes on the famous tree wasn't her intention. Far from it.

She took out a bill, then two, out of her wallet and put it in the donation box.

The man selling the wish kits gave her a grateful smile.

"Thank you so much," he said. "We appreciate your support. Would you like a kit?"

"No thanks." She smiled back at him. "I have everything I want." Why did she need to point that out? Stevie saw his gaze go from her to Ana, and back.

"All right then. Thanks again. You two have a great day."

"Did he just assume..." The glee to Ana's tone was unmistakable.

"Like all the others, yes, I think he did. It doesn't matter. It's true what I said. We came here so you could put yours on the tree, and that's what we're going to do. Those organizations do good work, no matter if the donation comes from a kit, or, well, a donation."

"I got you." Ana put an arm around her. "No voodoo, magic kind of stuff for Stevie. It's okay."

"I think voodoo is something else entirely."

"You're right. All I meant to say is I appreciate it too. It's still early. How about we get those gifts now?"

It wasn't a bad idea. Maybe all that shopping would tire Ana out, and Stevie would be able to sneak away and make that call.

"Yes, let's do it."

# Chapter Six

## ANA

A part of her wanted to believe so badly. Another part insisted that what she was doing was absurd, that she would know the likelihood of her wish coming true the moment she picked up the phone and asked her parents about holiday arrangements.

They hadn't explicitly said she wasn't welcome, but they had pointed out that Patricia wasn't. No point in telling them they weren't together anymore because it wouldn't solve the problem.

They had been wary of Stevie after her coming out, the sentiment expressed in thinly veiled jibes. Fortunately, at that time, they were already in college. If they didn't mention her, Ana didn't either, though something about this didn't sit right with her. Not just because she had figured out that she, too, liked women, and unlike Stevie, only women.

She had argued a few times, but eventually shut down to keep the peace. Ana wasn't proud of herself.

She couldn't find the right words yet, to write on that piece of paper, to say to her family or to Stevie, but she was determined to make a change. That was what Christmas was for, too, to be grateful for what you had, to identify where changes were necessary.

Rebirth.

Magic.

Hope.

Except at the moment, she was filling bags with gifts for her parents, brother and sister, her sister-in-law, and her nephew.

"On second thought, Aunt Carolyn and my cousin Gia might be there too, so I should have something for them."

Stevie looked thoughtful, and Ana had to ask.

"Is it too much, or simply too much to carry back to the inn?"

"It is...a lot," Stevie admitted. "But we can always take a cab."

"Thank you for being honest. I just can't help thinking...what if this is the last Christmas we all spend together?"

She loved Stevie for not pointing out the obvious. She didn't even know what would happen this Christmas.

"It's fine, really. We can grab lunch and call a cab after that. There's enough space in the room. Barely," she quipped. "But there's enough."

"Good. How about for lunch we try the diner Jo was talking about?"

"It's right across the street. Let's hit the chocolate store first, and then we can go?"

"Sounds great. I'll get something for Carolyn and Gia there."

She had bought Stevie's gift a while ago and brought it to give to her early. After the trip, they wouldn't see each other again until New Year's Eve. This gave her an idea. She might have to be quick and sneaky, but so be it. She owed Stevie a lot after this trip.

·▾·♥·♥·♥·▾·

Her plan had worked, and so, after leaving Chantal's Choco-latery, they went straight to the diner across the street. Inside, they found the same warm and festive atmosphere as in every business they had visited so far. Angel Falls might be a tourist attraction, but it was also a special place, no doubt about it.

The place was bigger than she had expected from the outside, the diner on the first floor, a winding staircase leading up to a café on the second. Somehow, they managed to straddle the line between modern and cozy. There was a counter for take-out.

"Let's check upstairs?" she suggested. "I think I could go for something sweet. What about you?"

"A sandwich, maybe. But let's see upstairs first."

Ana almost regretted making them climb all those stairs with the multiple bags, but she didn't anymore when they arrived on the second floor. Like the diner, the café was decorated, an electric fireplace at the far end adding to the cozy atmosphere. Stockings hung on each side, and at a closer look, Ana could see there was something in them.

In the space next to the window stood a decorated tree, like the one upstairs.

They chose a seat by the window close to the fireplace and tree, from which they could see the street bustling with shop-pers.

The task ahead wasn't an easy one, but she loved being here. There was something about Angel Falls that put her at ease. If only it could be Christmas all the time.

Ana got up to admire the ornaments on the tree. The arrangement was colorful and bright, traditional ornaments mixed with modern ones.

She smiled at the rainbow. Another one was heart-shaped in rainbow colors.

"Do you like it? I'm Leyla."

She turned around to realize she recognized Leyla from the restaurant the other day.

"Oh, I love it. It's beautiful. Do you work here?"

Not the smartest question to ask, but she still felt self-conscious for staring yesterday. Admiring. The purple hair color was even brighter up close.

"I do," Leyla said with a smile. "Actually, I own the place."

It wasn't until then that it registered with Ana that everyone working here had the same kind of nametag, including their pronouns. She appreciated that it helped her avoid another mistake.

"Wow, that's great! It's so cozy. I'm Ana, by the way, and this is my friend Stevie. We came to Angel Falls to put a wish on the tree."

She wasn't sure what part of that sentence made her blush harder, but Leyla seemed at ease either way.

"Like a lot of people," they affirmed. "I hope your wish will come true. What can I bring you?"

"I'll have the apple pie, please, with cream. And a latte. No, a white hot chocolate."

"What about you, Stevie?"

"I'll have the ham and cheese sandwich, and a latte. Thank you."

"You seem a little nervous," Stevie teased when Leyla was out of earshot.

"It's not about them," Ana hurried to clarify. She didn't want to give Stevie the wrong idea. "Though I wish I could rock that purple. No, it's just that—and I know it doesn't make any sense at all—I always get flustered when I'm around people who are so confident, who seem to have figured it all out? You know what I mean? It's not their fault, but it makes me feel inept, I guess."

"There's no reason. You are dealing with a lot right now, and you're still the same kind amazing person you've always been. I know you're good at your job too. Your kids love you, and they thrive when they're with you. I've seen it. In fact, I think you're the opposite of inept."

Leyla, who had brought their drinks and food, must have overheard Stevie's passionate speech.

"There you go. Enjoy."

Ana smiled, thinking it was a bit magic how Stevie managed to dissipate her doubts.

"Thank you. This looks delicious." The piece of pie was huge, but she didn't mind, since she knew she'd end up offering Stevie a part of it.

When they were out of earshot, Ana couldn't help returning to her point though.

"It's nice of you to say that, but...you do think I should handle things with my family differently."

"It doesn't matter what I think. Everyone is different. Everyone's family is different."

That wasn't an answer to the question, and Stevie apparently realized it. "To be honest? I don't know what I would do because I was never in your situation. I just think it's not fair to you. You gave them plenty of time. The next step should come from them."

If this was about anyone else, Ana would have whole-heartedly agreed with her.

"If I wait for that, I might lose them. And I can't risk that."

"I get it. You have a few days left. You'll make your wish, and by the way, you have more gifts in these bags than Santa. If they still don't appreciate you, f—"

"You're right." Ana wasn't concerned about the swear word Stevie might have intended to use, just the possibilities it evoked. "I have time. Once I've sorted everything out, I will write down my wish, and we can bring it to the tree later. Now, would you like to try that pie?"

"Please."

Stevie's expression at the first taste was pure bliss, making Ana smile despite the heavy subject.

They finished their meal and walked back to the inn.

Ana felt like having a nap, but instead, after putting away the gifts, she sat at the small desk and unpacked the kit. She took the small notepad the inn offered and started to write—no way she'd write on the blue paper without a draft.

*Dear Wishing Tree*...No, that sounded juvenile.

*My wish is*...What was it anyway? For her parents to accept her the way she was? To love her? Again? Still? Would a lack of conciseness interfere with the wish?

Ana shook her head to herself.

Mom, Dad, her brother Harrison, her sister Phoebe...Janelle, her sister-in-law, who had always been nice to her but never said much...Should she include her nephew who was too small to understand the conflict, and probably didn't care if she dated women, or just the adults? Janelle should be in the wish, too, she decided. She hadn't really offered her opinion, but she would likely side with Harrison. And what if Aunt Carolyn and her cousin Gia celebrated Christmas with them, did she have to mention them for it to work?

Before long, she was staring at five balled up pieces of paper, and she was no closer to finding the words.

The warm hand on her shoulder came out of nowhere.

"Is it possible that you're trying too hard?" Stevie asked softly. "Maybe just say how you feel. It's anonymous, so even if someone read this at some point, they would never know who it was from. That's the whole point, isn't it?"

"Yeah. I guess so. It's not that I'm worried about anonymity."

"Then go ahead and write from the heart. No one will edit you. There is no wrong way to do this."

How Stevie could be so calm and reasonable about something she didn't even believe in, Ana didn't know, but it did calm her too.

"Thank you." She sighed. "I thought I could do this quickly, but maybe I was wrong about that. I'm going to take a nap if you don't mind."

"Of course. How about I give you some time? I could hang out in the lobby for a bit, see if I have some emails to answer."

"You don't have to go."

"It's okay, really. I can tuck you in if you like."

It was most likely a joke, but when Ana took off her shoes and curled up on the bed, Stevie took the comforter and covered her with it.

"Sweet dreams," she said. "I'll be downstairs if you need me."

Part of her wanted to ask her to stay, but perhaps she should give Stevie a little room, too, since she was already going above and beyond. And maybe the solution would come to her in a dream.

◆ ◆ ◆ ◆ ◆

Ana did dream, though not about the perfect words to write on that light blue piece of paper. She was ice-skating with Stevie, her heart light and filled with warmth and gratitude. The whole scenery was doused in light, a familiar cast of characters with them: Jo, Leyla, the man who had sold them the wishing kit. She also saw her siblings, Stevie's Mom and Evan.

45

Her hand in Stevie's, she didn't feel the cold, even though neither of them was wearing gloves. They skated around the Christmas tree at the center of the ice rink, when Stevie stopped all of a sudden, turning to her.

Ana's heart was beating faster as the images started to fade and she inched closer to wakefulness.

She saw Stevie's face in front of her, her wide eyes, wisps of her hair that had escaped from her ponytail, framing a beautiful smile. Ana's gaze dropped to her lips, and then, hesitantly, she leaned in...only to wake up completely.

*What?* She realized she'd said it out loud, grateful that Stevie wasn't in the room. It wasn't such a big surprise, Ana reasoned. In the most difficult year of her life, Stevie had remained the only reliable constant. She wished it wasn't all about her new-found identity, but it was hard to escape when it was the very reason her family was at odds with her, and her ex-girlfriend had left her because she couldn't catch up in record speed. Or whatever was the right speed. Who knew?

The point was, she had enough on her plate without crushing on her best friend, the friend she desperately needed in her life.

Ana would never do anything to jeopardize that friendship, though she had to admit everything in that dream had felt good.

A glance at her phone told her that it had only been a little over ten minutes. She needed to nap a little longer, clear her head, and move forward.

Determined, she closed her eyes again.

# Chapter Seven

## STEVIE

Stevie said hi to Jo, who was working behind the reception counter, and chose an armchair far enough to have some privacy. Everything and everyone in this town was so warm and welcoming. If there was a pretense behind it, she hadn't found it yet, but that didn't mean it wasn't there, did it?

Perhaps her doubtful attitude was merely an attempt to protect herself, and more importantly, Ana, from getting their hopes up too high. Stevie had hopes too, even though most of them weren't for herself.

Finally, she clicked on the number she had saved well before their departure and waited. After three rings, one of the people she had intended to speak to picked up.

"Hello?"

"I'm sorry, wrong number," Stevie said quickly and ended the call. She could feel her face flush with embarrassment. She was an adult, on the right side of the argument. Why was this so hard? It shouldn't be.

She picked up her phone again, trying to channel all the Christmas spirit she could when Jo came by.

"Hi. I don't mean to disturb you..."

"That's fine! I wasn't really doing anything." Could she sound any more enthusiastic? *Coward*, she silently scolded herself.

"You are here for a few more days, right? Have you made plans besides the Wishing Tree?"

"Nothing specific," she answered.

"I don't know if you can make time, but I'm in a bit of a bind here. A volunteer for the toy drive has come down with the flu, and we're on a tight schedule as it is. Would you two be up for wrapping some gifts for a couple of hours this afternoon?"

Stevie let a few seconds pass by, baffled. This town wasn't for real, was it?

"I'm sorry if I overstepped. We don't normally put guests to work, but—"

"No, no, it's fine. I'm sure Ana will agree. Where does it take place?"

"It's not far from here, but I can drive you. We have some of the gifts to bring as well."

"I look forward to it," Stevie told her, and she couldn't have been more genuine. This sounded so much better than what she had been about to do, not that she was off the hook forever. At least, for a few hours.

"Really? Thank you so much!"

"I'll just go get Ana, and we can meet you downstairs."

She had no doubt that Ana would be happy to help out. What she hadn't told Jo was that only one of them was a good gift-wrapper, and it wasn't Stevie.

She'd do her best.

⋅♥⋅♥⋅♥⋅♥⋅♥⋅

48

As she had predicted, Ana was on board with helping the charity. She was quiet during the drive though, making Stevie wonder if she'd had nightmares, or a conversation with her folks back home. When Stevie asked, she denied.

"I'm good, just still a little sleepy. It will be good to have something to do."

With Jo around, Stevie didn't want to ask if she had made any progress drafting the wish, but she had seen no additional paper balls in the waste basket.

"Again, thank you so much," Jo said when she opened the door to the art gallery Stevie and Ana had visited earlier. "We have a couple of rooms in the back for storage and packing."

When they walked inside the area, Stevie shared a look with Ana, on her face an expression of amused disbelief.

Christmas music was playing while the eight people in the room were busy wrapping toys of all shapes and forms. One man in his seventies was wearing a Santa hat, two women in their twenties were in elf costumes, and everyone seemed in a fabulous mood.

"We had a lot of donations this year," Jo remarked. "That means many happy children."

"We're happy to help," Ana assured her. "So, we just pick a toy and wrap it?"

"That's Yvonne over there. She will get you started. Yvonne!"

Stevie recognized the woman as a server from the diner. She seemed to have come over from her shift, as she was still wearing her nametag with her name and pronouns.

"Hi. You must be Stevie and Ana? Let me show you your table."

The next two hours passed like minutes. Stevie couldn't help the goofy smile she knew she was wearing. The turn of events made her truly happy, giving her a chance to postpone the inevitable a bit longer.

While everyone was busy with the task at hand, they still exchanged a few words. Stevie and Ana learned that there were other tourists in the group, and among the volunteers who would distribute the gifts later.

"Does that make it more likely to make the wish come true?" Stevie wondered out loud, then wanted to slap herself. To her relief, no one took her question in jest.

"I don't think so," Tara said. "I made my wish ten years ago, and it came true."

Her husband Gavin sent her a smile. "I was lucky hers aligned with mine."

*Lucky you indeed.* Stevie didn't say it out loud, fearing it would sound petty. Maybe she was, just a little bit, petty and jealous, because everything seemed so easy for everyone around here.

She had gotten a few messages from the dating app but not answered any of them, realizing that she had too much to deal with at the moment. That didn't mean she wasn't longing for someone to be close to, someone who really got her. For the long run.

"So how did you two meet?" he asked while trying to fit a sheet of wrapping paper around a giant box of LEGOs.

"Oh, we're not...I mean..."

"Last year of high school," Ana intervened. "We had just moved for my dad's job, and I was miserable. Not only did I have to leave my friends behind, but I also didn't know anybody. Stevie was the first to talk to me, and I thought she was awesome...We've been together ever since."

Stevie shot her a surprised look, hoping to convey "what are you doing?" but Ana just smiled at her and said, "That counts for high school sweethearts, I think."

"It sure does," Tara confirmed. "Now, do I have to wrap this unicorn, or can I skip and put it in a gift bag?"

Everyone laughed, though Stevie couldn't help feeling like she had missed something. In the past, they hadn't always bothered correcting misconceptions, but they had never outright lied. Why now? Ana didn't look like she was feeling guilty at all, whistling along with the iconic Mariah Carey song as they continued to work.

And somehow, she was starting to relax too. Given what they were up against, maybe a little white lie that hurt no one, wasn't the worst thing. Stevie wasn't quite ready to admit it, but there might have been a time or two, over the years, when she had wished it could be true. More often, she had been proud that people would assume she could have a girlfriend like Ana, smart, caring and undeniably beautiful.

But she'd never said it out loud, not like this, because that would be weird.

After all the wrapping was done, Jo announced that she'd take all the volunteers to dinner at Leyla's diner, and they walked over to the place, this time staying on the ground floor.

Leyla was nowhere to be seen, but their staff seemed unfazed handling such a big group at the last minute. They pushed a couple of tables together, added some chairs, and somehow everyone had a nice seat with a view of the marketplace outside, or the tree, or other decorations.

Not that Stevie was focusing much on anything but Ana sitting across from her.

She couldn't let her down, especially not this year, not at Christmas. She was going to get over herself and do what she could to make Ana's wish come true. So much depended on it for her, Stevie was afraid to find out what would happen if it didn't work out somehow.

It shouldn't be so hard to appeal to someone's human decency if they were capable of love, even more so if that person claimed to take the holiday, and the meaning of Christmas, seriously?

Ana might be mad at her. She had an idea for a pre-emptive apology, and she silently thanked her parents for being creative when it came to traditions.

They would go home the day after tomorrow, but she had enough time to make it all happen. Her face flushed with an emotion she wasn't sure how to decipher. Excitement, for sure. Among other things.

"What are you thinking?" Ana leaned close as she whispered.

"Nothing important," Stevie lied. "Just...It's nice. All of this." At least that wasn't a lie. Most of the time, she had genuinely enjoyed her stay here, though she still was uncertain about that Wishing Tree attraction that had raised Ana's hopes so high.

It all looked pretty, but what if people invested too much in it? The town always ended up not only with donations for their charities, but also with lots of tourist money spent in restaurants and shops. What about the people whose stories didn't turn out like Tara and Gavin's?

"Then why are you frowning?" Ana, as observant as ever, asked.

"Am I? Sorry. I didn't mean to. I'm glad we could contribute."

"I'm sorry about earlier. You're not mad at me for not correcting to them, are you?" She was still whispering.

Truth be told, she had done a bit more than neglecting to correct the assumption, but there was only one answer Stevie could give.

"No. I'm honored, actually."

Ana blushed hotly, the realization making her own face heat. Before either one of them could say anything, Jo came to their end of the table.

"You two, I meant it when I said we don't usually have guests working. I'd like to offer you another night."

"That is very kind of you," Stevie said, casting an uncertain glance at Ana who was listening intently. "But we have to leave on the 23$^{rd}$."

"Do we?" Ana asked. "You're going to your mom's on the 26$^{th}$, right? I still have to check with Mom and Dad, but I don't think they expect me before Christmas Eve dinner. No, scratch that, it's even better if I don't arrive before dinner, because everyone will be mellow and in a good mood."

"Well, why don't you stay then?" Jo smiled, but Stevie thought she detected a hint of pain. Perhaps she had an inkling as to why Ana had come here, what kind of wish she'd write on the paper if she ever decided to do it. Maybe another day wasn't so bad for both of their plans.

"Are you sure?"

"If you don't have any other plans, I'm good." Ana shrugged.

"Me too. Thank you so much, Jo. We can pay for it though."

"I don't doubt that. But you won't," was Jo's cheery response. "Merry Christmas."

"Merry Christmas," they echoed.

·♥·♥·♥·♥·♥·

After the meal, the other volunteers started to leave. Stevie thought that Ana might want to return to their room to finally write down the wish, but instead she suggested moving up to the café.

"Would that be okay?" she asked Leyla who had come in for a late shift, waving to them.

"Yes, of course. Make yourselves comfortable. I'll be right up."

Stevie and Ana secured the same table they had sat at before, with the beautiful view. A comfortable warmth was emanating from the fireplace that was also a heater, music playing softly in the background.

"You are really okay?" Ana laughed, looking a bit self-conscious. "I'm not sure why I did that, but...I don't know, everyone was so happy and open-minded, I just wanted a part of it."

"I'm fine. And I meant what I said. "Stevie cleared her throat. "You are the most open-minded person I know. Don't ever let anyone tell you otherwise."

"I wish we could stay here all year, eating and drinking too much, and you complimenting me all the time."

"Just pointing out the truth, but I hear you." Somehow, she needed to bring them back to a lighter, funny ambience, the kind they were used to. Her face still felt hot. "At least we got another day."

"Yes, that's so nice of Jo."

"She's pretty nice," Leyla who had come to their table, commented. "Of course I'm biased, because she's also my aunt. What can I bring you?"

"The Baileys Mocha sounds amazing. How boozy is it?" Ana asked.

"Very," Leyla promised. "But since I know you don't have far to go, I recommend it."

"I'll have the same, then," Stevie confirmed.

They sat in comfortable silence, listening to the music, watching the snow fall outside, until Leyla returned with their orders. Each drink came with a heart-shaped cookie on the side.

"There you go."

"Thank you. These cookies look amazing."

"I can assure you they are. My pastry chef is madly talented," Leyla said before they headed downstairs again.

"No kidding," Stevie agreed, even though Leyla was already out of earshot. To Ana, she said, "Have you thought more about what to write for your wish?"

Ana took a sip of her coffee, ending up with a moustache of cocoa and whipped cream.

"Wow," she remarked.

Stevie's finger twitched, but before she could create a cheesy scene like from a real Christmas movie, Ana picked up her napkin and wiped her mouth.

"Yes, definitely boozy. And I'm not avoiding your question. I think you're right—I'll just go with a couple of sentences, something that feels right. I shouldn't take this so seriously, right? It's just an activity."

Her eyes were wide and pleading, and Stevie wasn't going to point out that they wouldn't have come all the way here for an "activity."

"It will be fine," she said. "I promise." This time she did reach out and took Ana's hand in hers. Ana didn't pull away.

"I know."

They sat like this for almost a minute before they went back to their drinks and Ana declared out of the blue, "I need the restroom. The only downside of this place is that it's downstairs."

"Well, we were downstairs earlier."

"Please, don't try to make me make sense."

They shared a smile before Ana left, and Stevie leaned back in her chair, trying to keep up with what was happening. What was about to happen. The latter sobered her up quickly. So far, the stay in Angel Falls had been easier than she had expected. The most difficult, yet necessary step was yet to come. For both of them.

She nearly called her mother to ask her for advice but decided otherwise. She had to see this through.

Before Ana returned, Leyla came back to add a few more ornaments to the tree.

"Gifts from customers," they explained as they turned to Stevie. "At this rate we might have to add another tree."

"Those ornaments are amazing," Stevie acknowledged. "I love the rainbow. I have to admit I was surprised..." She let her words trail off, unsure why she couldn't seem to keep her thoughts to herself today.

"Why would you be surprised?" Leyla asked. They came closer, pointing to an empty chair. "May I?"

"Of course. And I don't know, Angel Falls is...different from what I expected. Teaches you not to make assumptions, right? I'm still not entirely sure what to think. Everyone is so friendly. You don't always get that in a small town."

"You're right about that," Leyla acknowledged. "But Angel Falls is different, as you said. Everyone is welcome here."

"I'll admit, that was a relief. I'll also admit that I don't know what to think about this Wishing Tree business. My friend's family hasn't treated her kindly, and she's putting a lot of hope into this. Aren't you playing with people's emotions, selling it like that?"

Leyla wasn't offended by her direct approach. Good, because Stevie needed answers from someone.

"It's a valid question, and all of us here get it a lot. I can tell you this: Of course we need the tourists. At the end of the day, it helps us pay the bills and keep the lights on. But the rest, it's all real. We want this to be a place where people can take a breath, and if they want to, have a holiday like in the movies. It's for everyone. And most of them know that their wishes won't come true just like that," they snapped their fingers, "but they find a moment of peace, to reflect and figure out where they want to go next."

"That makes a lot of sense."

"I hope so." Leyla laughed. "We've been doing this for a while. I promise you, it works. But then it's really simple—we try to be kind whenever we can and get out of the way when we can't. I hope your friend can find that peace. And you too."

"Oh, I'm just here for her," Stevie felt the need to correct. "I don't even celebrate Christmas. Much. But this is important to her, and so…"

"She means a lot to you."

"I love her. As a friend, I mean. We've been best friends forever."

Leyla smiled enigmatically. "She's lucky to have you," they said before getting up to leave.

Ana returned at that moment, declaring, "How about another one of those magical mochas?"

Stevie couldn't say no to her, though she knew one thing without a doubt: She was the lucky one.

# Chapter Eight

## ANA

High school sweethearts? Why did she say that? Ana considered herself lucky that Stevie was this easygoing, not bothered by her small transgressions. She wasn't sure what had triggered them, but she knew this: Angel Falls felt like a warm hug, one she needed badly. Everyone they had met had affirmed her hopes, Jo, Leyla, Gavin and Tara. Here, no one made it complicated, and with Stevie by her side, she felt like she could do anything.

Convey to her family that there was nothing wrong with her, that she was capable of having and giving love, of having a family of her own one day, friends and neighbors who respected her. Ana loved the kids in her class, but she wouldn't mind having one of her own someday. If she met the right person to parent them with...

To some extent, her wish had already come true. No one here judged her. If only that could apply to her loved ones back home as well.

When it was Stevie's turn to go to the bathroom, Leyla came by with a stack of flyers.

"I heard you'll still be here tomorrow, so if you feel like it, come by in the afternoon."

"A cookie decorating contest?"

Leyla laughed. "Sure, we do that here."

"You know, ever since I stepped foot into Angel Falls, I feel like I've been dreaming. You are all too good to be true."

"It's a beautiful place," her host agreed, "but I promise you it can be messy too. This," they indicated the flyer, "will definitely be messy, and a lot of fun."

"It's not just for children?"

"Oh no, it's for everyone who wants to give it a try."

"Perhaps we'll be there then."

"Cool. See you there."

Alone again, she checked her phone. Nothing from her parents or siblings, but her aunt Carolyn had sent a text and asked if she'd be at Christmas Eve dinner. She'd answer her later, or maybe call tomorrow. Her sister-in-law, Janelle, had sent a cute virtual Christmas card with a baby reindeer.

She would likely see her the day after tomorrow too. Already. She wasn't ready. At least it wouldn't be as awkward as the times when she had brought Patricia, but it might be awkward, nonetheless.

At least little Jayden would present the perfect buffer, channeling most of the attention. Did she have enough gifts for him? She was certain that the wooden train set she had found here in Angel Falls would make him happy. He might not care much about the clothes, so she had added a few sweets. Not too many, because the parents might not like that.

Complicated. She sighed, but had to smile at the same time, because she was still in Angel Falls with Stevie, sipping boozy hot chocolate in a diner where no one felt left out, or worse, mocked or openly rejected.

For the moment, life was good.

"My turn. What are you thinking?" Stevie asked after she'd returned from the bathroom.

"Do we have to go home? I mean, ever?"

"Honestly? At some point, yes, but not yet. Do you want to walk around a bit more before we go back to the inn?"

"Sure."

That might be optimistic, given the amount of alcohol they'd had, but Ana was always up for an adventure when Stevie was the one asking. And as Leyla had pointed out, they wouldn't have to go far.

They paid at the counter and said goodbye before stepping out in the cold.

The market was still open, and on the Wishing Tree, colorful envelopes encased in their bubbles swayed gently in the wind.

They stopped at the merry-go-round and watched the passengers, children and adults projecting unadulterated happiness. Before she could even form the words, Stevie went up to the booth and bought two tickets. When the ride had ended and everyone got off, she chose a carriage and stepped onto the side of the carousel, reaching out a hand.

"My lady...Your chariot awaits."

Ana giggled and took her hand, following her to the seat.

"This is perfect. How do you always know what I need before I even say it?"

"Special talent." Stevie put an arm around her shoulders. "You know, I appreciate what my parents were trying to do, but when you don't observe certain dates, you sometimes miss events."

"And when you take them too seriously, they can give you a giant stress headache."

They both laughed as the merry-go-round began to move, children on colorful wooden horses squealing with delight.

This close, she was much aware of the scent of Stevie's perfume, the moment unusually intimate and exciting. Maybe Christmas wouldn't get much better than this. She might not get everything she wanted, but she had so much, didn't she?

It would be greedy to want more. From Stevie anyway.

But it turned out Stevie had even more to give to her.

They wandered home, and when they were back in their room, Ana sat down to write a quick note on the blue paper, folded it and slid it into the envelope, before she closed the two halves of the clear globe around it.

"There, all done," she declared. "We can go and put it up before breakfast tomorrow."

"Perfect."

It was. The most important task done, Ana went to the bathroom. When she returned, she couldn't believe her eyes. If the room had been over the top Christmassy before, Stevie had turned it up a few notches. She had lit all the lights and LED candles in the room, and there were presents under the small tree in the corner. The TV screen was paused on what looked like the beginning of a Christmas movie.

"What is all this?" she asked, and Stevie turned a hopeful gaze on her.

"Christmas," she said. "I know it's not the date yet, but I won't see you until New Year's Eve, so...I thought we could do it now."

"Wow. This is...It's amazing. Thank you so much!" She all but leapt into Stevie's arms, nearly tackling her onto the bed. Wow. Did she really have that much to drink? And why would that dream come back to her at the worst possible moment?

Stevie was being a terrific friend. She didn't need to know how much Ana loved being close to her, at night when they somehow always ended up cuddling, during the day when they never ran out of things to talk about, when they could talk about everything.

"But wait a second. I have a gift for you too. Well, two actually."

"We can start with one tonight, and the rest tomorrow if you prefer."

"No. If you're okay with it, I want them tonight. I can be unconventional too, and it's only the 22$^{nd}$, after all."

"All right then." Stevie waited until Ana had unearthed two packages from her suitcase and put them with the other ones. "Start with this?" she asked.

Ana sat on the bed, legs folded underneath her, and tore away the paper from the square soft package Stevie had handed her, to reveal a lovely surprise.

"You're not saying anything? Too much?" Stevie sounded nervous, and she nearly tackle-hugged her again.

"No, not at all. I always wanted matching PJs!"

That threw her friend for a loop. "And in almost eight years, you never said a thing? I could have done this so much sooner! That means...you like them?"

"I love them," Ana confirmed. "And we didn't exactly spend Christmas together before, so how would you know?"

She took the light blue and white nightwear out of the package and pulled her sweater over her head.

"Um...what are you doing?"

"Trying them on. Isn't that what they are for, to be worn before there are more gifts?"

"Okay...I guess."

Ana was already out of her pants when she noticed that Stevie hesitated. They had always been comfortable around each other. Had something changed? Had she crossed a line by making Stevie an accomplice to this endeavor?

But no, Stevie had set up the room to celebrate Christmas early.

"Come on. It will be more fun when we watch the movie."

"Yes, definitely." Finally, Stevie changed as well, and Ana couldn't keep the grin off her face. It might be silly and cheesy, but she thought it was adorable above all. Stevie's PJs had the same snowflake pattern, just with a dark top and lighter bottoms.

"This is so cute," she gushed. "Now open one of mine, okay?"

Given the fact that her friend had put three packages under the tree, she was glad to have bought the package from the chocolatery.

Stevie's eyes lit up when she uncovered the bag of hand-made truffles in the set with a small book full of chocolate related recipes.

"That is so sweet!"

"Yeah, that's me. And I bet they are too."

"We have to try them later," Stevie insisted. "Your turn."

The next gift was a bit heavier, and Ana made an educated guess based on the shape and weight.

"You said you still enjoy paperbacks. I read these recently and thought you might enjoy them."

"I'm sure I will. That's awesome. You have to be reading my mind."

Not that she did, not really, Stevie was just a really good listener.

Ana smiled to herself, hoping she had done as well.

"I remember that conversation," she said. "We both said we needed to clean up our e-readers, because there are so many of them...but sometimes it's really fun to hold a book in your hands."

She picked up another package she had brought from home, a couple of books for Stevie this time.

"It is. Wow. Thank you. Those were literally next on my list."

It was funny how Stevie had gotten her into mysteries, and for a few months now, Stevie had started to pick up romance more often.

"I'm just sad I have only two gifts for you. You did all this…" She made a gesture indicating the room, where the picture on the TV was still frozen.

"It's not that much," Stevie insisted. "Just one more, and we can watch the movie. Actually, I found a couple, if it's not too late for you."

"Not at all. We can sleep in a bit tomorrow, since we don't have to leave yet."

"That's a great idea." Ana reached for the remaining gift bag and took out her gift encased in a small package, significantly smaller than the others. "Now, what could this be?"

Was Stevie really giving her jewelry? And why did that make her heart beat this fast?

There was indeed a necklace in the small box, the pendant a silver outline of an angel. Ana had admired them at the market the other day.

"This is perfect," she said, her cheeks warm, but she didn't mind. "No matter what happens, I'll never forget our time here."

Was there a hint of wistfulness to Stevie's smile?

"That was the plan," she said. "How about some bubbles now?"

"I definitely feel like celebrating those awesome gifts. And these surroundings…I had imagined it would be beautiful, but it's so much more."

"Good."

"First, let me put this on." She fumbled with the clasp for a second or so until Stevie reached out to fasten it while Ana held her hair up. She couldn't suppress the small shiver when Stevie's fingers brushed the back of her neck.

Yes, this Christmas was already perfect.

They finally opened the truffles, and the champagne Stevie produced from the small fridge, and started the movie, a sweet romcom first, *Carol* after that, and Ana couldn't help thinking how incredibly lucky she was. Something had clearly changed from when she had first decided that there was no way around it, that she *needed* to go to Angel Falls and participate in their Christmas tradition.

She would still hang her ornament on the Wishing Tree, and she still hoped above all that she could be part of a family, *her* family, again. And there was another wish, hope, fantasy forming in her mind, one that no Christmas magic could ever make come true, because that would be too much to ask for.

She already had so much.

She couldn't banish the thought from her mind, eased by champagne, watching fictional love stories, and the fact that she appreciated the woman next to her beyond measure.

Loved. She had always loved Stevie for making her feel at home, for making her feel that she was enough, but it was hard to deny any longer. Something else had been added to the equation. Her cheeks were burning when the couple in the second movie kissed, quite chastely, for the first time.

It might be coincidence, wishful thinking or intent, but Stevie turned at the same time she did, and for a few seconds, they just stared into each other's eyes, their lips nearly touching.

How had this never happened before? How had she not known how much she wanted it to happen...

Stevie sat back, and she said, "It's about time."

It took Ana a moment to realize she was talking about the couple on the screen, not them.

Her stomach lurched a bit, too many indulgences, too many revelations, and she still had to figure out Christmas. Had she gone too far?

But Stevie didn't seem worried or offended, just pensive.

"I'm sorry." The words were out before she could even contemplate the right ones.

"No. No, it's all good. We're good."

Stevie reached out to tuck a strand of hair behind her ear, the tender gesture feeling so right and wrong at the same time, Ana wanted to cry. Make it clear that she wasn't just drunk, or desperate, that this wasn't a spur of the moment thing. But the window of opportunity had come and gone. She took another sip of her now flat champagne.

It didn't look like that other wish would come true, but at least Stevie would still be her friend. As always. The rest, she'd get over it, even though the disappointment made her eyes sting.

# Chapter Nine

## STEVIE

S tevie wanted to slap herself for not finding the courage earlier. Ana might have talked it out with her parents by now, and they could have...what? Followed this new exciting path in their relationship? The thought was more than thrilling, but Stevie wasn't sure she could, or should.

No matter how much she had wanted to kiss Ana, something that felt still mildly bewildering, and yet made so much sense. She had told Leyla that she loved Ana, and that was nothing but the truth.

But there was something she had to do first, and if she waited any longer, the window of opportunity would slam shut in her face.

She would explain everything to Ana at the right time.

While she was still asleep, Stevie extracted herself once more from her embrace and silently got dressed before she went downstairs.

She went back to that armchair in the corner. The breakfast service was already in progress, and delicious smells made her stomach rumble.

Stevie clicked the same number, and when the phone was answered this time, she spoke.

"Hi, Mrs. Blake. This is Stevie, Ana's friend."

"Of course I remember you. How are you?"

"I'm fine, thank you."

The Blakes had always been polite, even though Stevie knew that they were wary of her. She could handle the latter. There would be no yelling.

"If you wanted to talk to Ana, I'm afraid she's not here."

"Yes, I know. I was hoping I could have a word with you. I promise I won't bother you for long, but it's Christmas, and it's really important to Ana."

"Well, if it was, she wouldn't go out of her way to make a mess of her life, and would care about her family a bit more, wouldn't she?"

At that point, Stevie wanted to yell, but she reined in the impulse.

"Ana is the most put together person I know. And she cares so much. All she wants is to be sure that you still love her."

"What the heck is this?" Mrs. Blake asked, now suspicious. "If this is so important to her, why isn't she the one calling?"

*Because she's here with me to put a wish on a tree, as a last resort.*

"I know you've had some arguments lately, but I'm asking you, please don't turn her away. There is nothing wrong with her. She's still the same person, kind, funny, and amazing, and if you look into your heart, you will see that."

Stevie cringed hard at her choice of words, though on second thought, she found nothing untrue about them.

"You have no idea what you are talking about," Mrs. Blake scoffed. "We love Ana, of course we do, that's why we want to keep her from throwing her life away."

"The life you wanted for her. Doesn't it count at all what she wants?"

"How dare you speak to me this way? You think you know better than her family what's good for her?"

"No, you misunderstood, I didn't mean—"

"I understood you fine. You're the one who put all those ideas in her head."

"That's not true. Please, hear me out—"

The other woman hung up on her, and Stevie sat, feeling like she'd been slapped. Jo walked by and stopped.

"Are you all right?"

"I'm not sure," she admitted. "I was trying to fix something, and I'm afraid I made it worse. No, I know I did. Much worse." She should have asked Ana's mother to keep quiet about the conversation, though she doubted it would have made a difference. "I'm sorry, I have to go."

"See you at breakfast, then."

Stevie didn't wait but hurried up the steps to their room. She needed a couple of attempts to open the door with the keycard, her heart sinking when she saw Ana toss her phone aside. Her gaze was stormy.

"What the hell did you do?"

So much for plan A. It had looked so good in theory. Ana's parents would listen and call her to let her know that she was welcome, at Christmas and always. What planet had she lived on? How had she ever imagined that the Blakes would easily be convinced to give up their prejudice?

"I'm so, so sorry," she tried. "I knew it was your wish. I wanted it to come true for you so much."

"Well, you did the exact opposite," Ana snapped. She put her coat over her PJs.

"You're not going to go out like this? Can we please talk about this?"

"No, we can't." With an exaggerated huff, Ana took off her bottoms and replaced them with jeans and socks before she bound her hair in a loose ponytail. Next, she put on her boots.

"Ana."

"No. I can't talk to you right now. Don't come after me."

She slammed the door on her way out, and Stevie slumped onto the bed, letting the tears fall.

Ana was right: She had ruined everything. *Figures*. She knew nothing about Christmas magic or dealing with families who couldn't see past their prejudice.

She had overstepped, thinking she could somehow make things right when the truth had been so obvious all along. Now, Ana was angry with her on top of mourning the loss of relationships, and the whole reason why they'd come here, a moot point. It was all tainted now, and it was Stevie's fault.

And here she was, feeling sorry for herself.

She thought that her parents had been right about Christmas all along.

·♥·♥·♥·♥·♥·

Stevie wished there was someone she could text, *Help! I messed up!* to someone who would really understand, but deep in her heart she knew that person had always been the one she had hurt without meaning to.

The atmosphere in Angel Falls had been getting to her, melting away her cynicism. She was still angry at Ana's parents who made it so hard for Ana to feel loved. Most of all she was angry at herself though, because she should have known better, regardless of her good intentions.

She didn't have much of an appetite either, so she bundled up, left the inn, and walked back to the marketplace, not sure what she hoped to find there.

And they'd still have to drive home tomorrow.

Would they both be spending Christmas alone?

# Chapter Ten

## ANA

S he couldn't believe Stevie had done this to her, had gone behind her back when all this time, she acted like she trusted Ana to make decisions and handle her family on her own.

Her mother had been furious, and while she didn't say it in so many words that everyone thought Ana should stay away, the message had come across, loud and clear.

Not that Ana felt like joining a group of people that felt like strangers to her, that treated her like a suspicious stranger, because she dared to be herself. She had never shared it with Stevie, but a year ago she had sometimes wondered if she could simply make it go away, until she realized it wasn't rational or possible.

Now everything was broken.

Christmas. Their friendship. The hope that the trip to Angel Falls could make any difference whatsoever.

Ana walked in angry strides, oblivious to the beauty around her she had admired just yesterday, the lights and decorations.

Kind and happy people. It was an illusion, all of it. It had to be, because life was so much more complicated.

The snow mingled with the tears on her face as the realization sank in: She had nowhere to go. Not just for Christmas. And she could see it all so clearly now: Her family had stayed polite, because it didn't take a genius to see that Patricia wasn't the one for her. They treated her like a brief, unpleasant, somewhat embarrassing phase in Ana's life, the memory making her cringe even now. Patricia hadn't been right for her, for sure, and she had been patronizing at times. That didn't mean Ana shouldn't have stood up for her more.

Stevie's actions had a more severe impact, because all her family was aware that she was a constant in Ana's life.

Had been.

She cried harder as she continued along Main Street, unaware of concerned looks thrown her way.

Last night, she had felt free, and life had been full of possibilities, magic even. For a brief moment, when she thought that Stevie was going to kiss her. Ana wasn't sure how much more she could bear to lose.

But she couldn't be around her either, not now.

Ana felt queasy, though she couldn't say if it stemmed from the—once again—chaotic situation she found herself in, or an overindulgence of food and drink the night before.

It seemed so pointless now to put that ornament on the Wishing Tree when she had already gotten such a harsh reality check.

At least she'd made a small contribution to make someone else's Christmas better, and that was worth something, wasn't it?

She arrived at the tree, the lights and colors blurring as she couldn't stop crying. Ana turned away quickly when she saw a familiar face, one of the other guests with his young daughter. She wasn't quick enough.

"What happened? Do you need help?" he asked, concerned. The little girl was holding on to his hand, sending him a questioning look.

"I need help all right," Ana said, and then she couldn't help laughing.

No, definitely not the reaction to dispel someone's worries.

"Why don't we get out of the cold, and you tell me about it?" he offered. "Cassie and I were just about to get a hot chocolate at the diner. How about you join us?"

"Oh no." At least she had her voice under control now. "I don't want to impose." Most of all, she wanted Stevie, but she couldn't forgive the betrayal, at least not yet. It didn't matter that any of Ana's attempts to address the situation would have likely led to the same result. At least, that would have been her own doing. It would have made all the difference.

"You're not. We have to wait for my husband, and I think we've been to every shop and booth twice—if not more. I get it," he said as they walked a few steps. "Christmas is the most wonderful, and the most stressful time of the year."

"Tell me about it."

Ana wondered how his, and his husband's family had reacted when they came out to them—or told them that they were going to start their own family. Or, if they were still on speaking terms at all.

Stevie had a point: Why was it so hard for some people to just let others be? Why did her parents have to be "some people?" She was exhausted from it all, now truly embarrassed that she had drawn a stranger's sympathy, and that she had believed a tree would somehow change the trajectory of important relationships.

"I'm okay, really," she said, the loud noise her stomach made suggesting otherwise, making Cassie crack up. "Okay, I might have run out before breakfast, but I had a reason. I think. I could go for one of their pastries, but you don't have to sit with me."

She might have been too obvious hoping that they would.

"That's okay. I'm Toby," he said.

"Ana. All right."

They walked the few steps to the diner, and much to her relief, he didn't ask about her crying fit at the Wishing Tree, just made conversation about his family and their trip to Angel Falls. Whenever he asked a question, they were non-invasive and more general, and Ana managed to calm down somewhat, which was in no small part due to the tasty breakfast.

Leyla gave her a smile when they brought their orders, but fortunately they didn't comment on Ana's appearance, or Stevie's absence.

"Everyone is so open and accepting here," Toby said. "I wish we could bring some of that home with us. I mean, it's okay where we live, but Angel Falls is pretty much perfect."

"Too good to be true."

"You think?"

"Well, we can't take it home," Ana argued. "And we can't stay here forever. There will always be people who don't understand, and for the most part, we can ignore them. It's a little harder when it's people we love."

"No doubt about it." He ruffled his daughter's curls gently. "That makes a big difference."

Silence ensued, and Ana realized that he was giving her the opportunity to elaborate.

"I don't want to talk about it. It would ruin my appetite."

That, and the person who had always been first on her call list, for better or worse, was not available right now. She sighed.

"I don't want to be rude either, but...It's complicated. To say the least."

"No problem."

Toby unobtrusively changed the subject to a safer one, and they both shared about the job they'd be returning to after the holidays. Well, safe within a certain perimeter, she thought. One of her colleagues identified as a lesbian and had brought her wife to a bake sale, so Ana didn't think she'd have a problem there. Not that she had ever said anything, because her relationship with Patricia hadn't been long enough.

It was Stevie who had sometimes picked her up after work, who had been with her a few times when they ran into co-workers.

She almost laughed again, but resisted the impulse because Toby might have called in help—but realistically, how many of those co-workers had thought she and Stevie were together, never saying a word?

She couldn't escape her anywhere.

Yesterday, Ana wouldn't have thought this was a problem, now everything was upside down, too close, too far, she couldn't seem to get it right.

But she couldn't stay here with a sympathetic stranger forever either.

"I'll still see you later?" Leyla asked when they came by with the bill.

Ana gave them a blank look until she realized what Leyla was talking about. She doubted she'd be in the mood to decorate cookies, but at least it would give her an excuse to avoid Stevie.

·♥·♥·♥·♥·♥·

After thanking Toby and Cassie for their company, she went to wash her face in the restroom and walked back to the hotel. Stevie wasn't there, which was a relief. She had sent a text though, Ana realized.

*I am so sorry. I went to take a walk, but my phone is on if you need to reach me. Please just let me know if you're okay.*

*I'm fine*, she sent back, so Stevie wouldn't come looking for her. She'd know it was a lie, but Ana didn't see an alternative. Not yet. So much had happened at once, the only thing she knew with certainty was that she couldn't take it on all at once.

One step at a time. Her gaze fell on the ornament ready to be hung on the tree, tears threatening to fall again when she remembered writing down the wish, from the heart, as Stevie had advised.

The room was still slightly messy from yesterday's activities, their pre-Christmas celebration and gift-giving. She picked up one of the three books Stevie had given her, and then she realized she was still wearing the PJ top. And the angel necklace. She touched it with her fingertips, remembering how happy it had made her only yesterday.

"You do need help," she said out loud. Not the kind her parents thought she required, for sure, but she wouldn't mind some advice, someone telling her what to do. It looked like she was extraordinarily bad at figuring it out for herself and trusting the right people.

No, that wasn't entirely true.

Stevie had meant well, even though she had made a mess of things.

Unintentionally. The mess remained, and someone had to clean it up.

Ana checked her phone again, but as expected, no one other than Stevie had tried to contact her.

She started a text message to her mother.

*I'm really sorry about Stevie. Can we talk about it tomor-row...*She deleted the text and tossed the phone aside. If she went out again to join Leyla for the cookie decorating, she might as well shower and change first. She tried to remember if she had taken off her coat at the diner earlier and sat there wearing the cute PJ top she had gotten for Christmas.

Talk about messy. She could do better. She would.

On second thought, she would bring the ornament as well. It sure wouldn't help now, but it wouldn't do any more harm either.

·♥·♥·♥·♥·♥·

The snow had stopped, crunching under her boots as she took the same path back to Main Street. There was a line at the booth, and she stood and watched a bit, people talking and laughing, some of them writing their wish and putting it on the tree right there.

A sense of sadness and disappointment washed over her when she realized that once again, she felt left out. Angel Falls was supposed to be different. The problem was, she hadn't changed. She was still afraid.

But she had put on some make-up, and she was determined not to cry. Not again.

"Here goes nothing," she mumbled and put the ornament on the highest branch she could reach, for no particular reason.

She watched a couple she had seen earlier at the diner, put up their wishes. Toby and his husband were there too, and he was holding up Cassie for her to hang her ornament. Ana ducked away, not wanting to be seen this time. She turned away and walked back to the diner where a substantial space had been cleared for the event.

As expected, most of the participants were children, but a number of adults were trying their luck too. As she was looking for a place to sit, she recognized one of them too late.

"Hi," Stevie said, looking chastised. She had a cookie and some icing in front of her. Until today, Ana would have cracked a joke about modern art, and then sat down and showed her some piping tricks, but that was in the past, or was it?

She couldn't get over the fact that Stevie didn't trust her to get it right. That made her no different from Patricia, didn't it? And why would she be the expert anyway? Her parents had accepted her unconditionally, in and out of the closet.

Since there was no other place, she got herself a kit and sat down.

Realizing she wouldn't get much conversation out of Ana, Stevie turned to her cookie. And back to Ana.

"Look, I understand you're mad. You have every right to be."

"That's right. We can stop there. I don't really want to discuss this here." Or ever. Her chest tightened when Stevie's face fell. When had she become such an unpleasant person to be around?

Inept.

"Okay," Stevie said softly. "I understand."

"I don't think you do, but let's just get this over with, shall we?"

That wasn't what she had meant to say either, but after that, Stevie didn't try to engage her any longer and instead focused on the task at hand.

Ana did too, creating intricate snowflake patterns on her cookies while stealing glances at her friend with a heavy heart.

She had never been good at finding the right words, expressing what was on her mind. Making her parents understand why she still deserved to be loved, Patricia, why she had to do massively important things at her own pace...She always felt like she had to catch up, say more, elaborate more, with very little impact. Except with Stevie. Often, they didn't even need words, finishing each other's sentences like an old married couple. Other times, Stevie knew exactly what she wanted to say even before Ana.

But not this time.

She was wrong this time, and it came at a cost, for Ana, maybe for Stevie too, if Ana's friendship still meant anything to her.

She still wanted to kiss her. Talk about being a lousy communicator.

"Wow," Leyla commented as they walked by. "You're an artist."

Turns out, she was a much better cookie decorator.

Ana blushed. "They're okay."

"She's always been so good at this." Stevie's expression held mild alarm, as if she thought Ana would object to her speaking up.

"I can see that. We might have to keep you in Angel Falls and hire you as a cookie decorator. We make them all year long."

For the first time today, Ana's laugh was genuine.

"You are too kind. I'm not that good."

"You are. Trust me."

An employee called for Leyla, and they left. Ana couldn't ignore Stevie's gaze on her, longing and a bit desperate. She still looked amazing, her eyes a bit red-rimmed, as if she had cried too.

Ana felt torn between anger and the realization that she had come here the same...longing and desperate.

"You shouldn't have done this."

"I know."

"That doesn't make it better though. The damage is done. There was yelling for about ten minutes, now no one is calling me back. Looks like they're done." She needed Stevie to understand what she had done, but she couldn't stand her look of despair either. "I know that wasn't your intention, and that

Christmas Eve might have ended badly anyway. I know all of that. It still wasn't your decision to make."

"I know..."

"You went behind my back, made me feel like I couldn't do what needed to be done. Like you knew better."

"I didn't, and I never meant to make you feel that way. I got carried away..."

"Yeah."

Tara, who had wrapped gifts with them for the toy drive, came by their table to say hello, and it was a welcome interruption.

Ana wished she could move to another table, or just leave, but she didn't want...What? Was she still that worried about what other people thought of her, people she would never see again?

Sad. Pathetic.

Inept.

She continued to frost her cookies, and soon a group formed around their table, people complimenting her.

"Excuse me," Ana said and got up.

Looking alarmed, Stevie got to her feet as well.

"Do you mind if I go back to the inn with you?"

"Feel free. It's your room too," she said, not caring who overheard, and walked away.

# Chapter Eleven

## STEVIE

Perhaps she had always understood, to some extent, that her actions were wrong, and that she put their friendship on the line. At the time, it had seemed like an acceptable risk, if she could make Ana happy, if she could save Christmas for her.

She had achieved the complete opposite. Stevie couldn't care less if Mr. and Mrs. Blake never spoke to her again, but Ana being distant and aloof hurt. A lot, mostly, because she resented herself for going at this all wrong.

Now she was walking a few steps behind her like a stalker, which wasn't any better.

What if she never forgave her?

Ana briefly stopped at the Wishing Tree before she turned back to walk in the direction of the inn, and for a lack of a better idea, Stevie followed her.

She had noticed Ana had changed out of the PJ top she'd worn this morning, and into a blouse. Chances were she didn't want those PJs, or the books, or anything from Stevie any longer, even if yesterday, there had been a moment...a thin line to cross into new, uncharted territory, a split-second that left her longing and wanting.

Stevie had made her choices, and they were the wrong ones.

If Ana wanted to go home today, they could still make it before dinner.

She was going to suggest that as a peace offering.

Ana reached the inn before her, walking up the illuminated steps and went inside.

Stevie hesitated. She thought of the many gifts Ana had bought, hopeful that her family would not only accept them, but her as well. What would happen to them? Not that it mattered, not really.

She straightened her shoulders and entered the inn, finding Jo behind the reception counter as usual, chatting and laughing with guests that were checking out. Perhaps their wish had come true, and now they were going home to spend Christmas Eve, or Christmas Day, with their families.

What she had learned about Angel Falls was still true: The community was so kind and welcoming, it was truly miraculous. That didn't mean that everyone's dream could come true.

Ana's. Or Stevie's. That's what she got for keeping things from her best friend.

How much she had wanted to make things right for her.

That she was falling in love with her, had been steadily, for some time now.

What a moment to come to the realization.

Her timing couldn't have been worse.

·♥·♥·♥·♥·♥·

Ana was watching TV, a repeat of a crime drama, when she entered the room.

The evidence of Stevie's attempt at providing Christmas was still all over the place, wrapping paper, the gifts they had exchanged. Glasses. They had forgotten to change the sign from "Do Not Disturb" to "Please Clean the Room."

"Do you want to go home? We could pack up and go now," she offered.

"No," Ana said, not taking her eyes off the screen.

"I thought you might prefer—"

Finally, Ana looked up at her.

"If it's all the same to you, I'd prefer to stay as planned. I think I'll read a bit."

"Of course. Look, I understand you hate me right now, but—"

"I could never hate you," Ana said, her features softening some. Her words, nevertheless, were final, igniting a glimmer of hope.

"Could we—"

"Not now, Stevie." The defensive tone was back. It would take more than an apology to win Ana's trust back, but Stevie wouldn't give up trying. As long as it took. As long as there was something between them that she could still save. It would mean everything.

She picked up one of her own books and started reading. Stevie found it hard to concentrate with Ana next to her, sad, silent. Beautiful. Somehow, that had always been on her mind, from the moment Ana Blake walked into that literature class and they shared a smile as she walked to her desk. Stevie's appreciation had been so instant, and constant, that she never stopped to question it, never analyzed what it really meant.

Now, it might be too late.

⋆ ⋆ ♥ ⋆ ♥ ⋆ ♥ ⋆

Attraction, miscommunication, her book did nothing to distract her. Stevie's gaze kept going to Ana who appeared to be engrossed in her own read, as if drawn by an invisible force.

"What is it?"

She didn't sound mad anymore, just tired.

"Would you like a truffle?"

Ana considered Stevie's offer, which was more than she had expected, and it made her brave. Maybe foolishly so.

"I could go downstairs and get us a hot chocolate to go with them?"

"No," Ana declined so swiftly it made her flinch. "I mean, I'll have one of those, thank you. But if I have one more hot chocolate, I'll never want another one for the rest of my life."

Her delivery was so matter of fact that Stevie couldn't hold back the laughter, and Ana smiled. They had snickered at the sweet Christmas movie where characters drank enough hot cocoa to make a person nauseated. That seemed like forever ago. She wished they could return to that sense of ease.

She should have known better. Done better. But for now, she had to respect Ana's wish not to address the subject.

"No hot chocolate, got it." She went to get the truffles she had put into the mini-fridge the other night.

"Thanks." Ana picked one and went back to her book.

Stevie tried to do the same, but she couldn't make it work.

"Would you mind if I went out for a bit? I'll have my phone in case you need me, and I'll be back for dinner."

"Sure, no problem."

That did sting a little, but it was a reasonable course of action. Ana needed time and space in which she didn't have to think about anything. Stevie needed time and space to think.

Something drew her back to the Wishing Tree, the reason Ana had decided she had to go to Angel Falls, which was the reason Stevie had dropped everything to come with her.

Ana was right—she had wildly overstepped. Not just because she had spoken to her mother without her consent, but she had been the worst kind of patronizing, assuming Ana truly thought a tree had the power to change stubborn minds.

And what if it did? Stevie still didn't believe it, not really, but it was up to Ana what she wanted to believe or not. She hadn't asked Stevie to fix anything, just to be there with her.

That was something so self-evident that Stevie felt she had to go above that, do something to make that wish come true, when all she needed to do was to be a friend, be present. Listen.

She wanted to tell her that she truly understood it now, but Stevie also understood it was too early to raise the subject. She hoped that eventually, she could make her case to Ana, apologize again, tell her that she would take back her actions if she could.

At this moment, there was no line at the booth, and she went and purchased a kit, hers a bright yellow.

Stevie wasted no time, searched her purse for a pen, found one and scribbled a couple of sentences on the paper she put into the matching envelope. Then she hung it on the tree, amazed to find the action calming and exciting alike. Like buying a lottery ticket when you knew the chances were smaller than slim, but still, it could happen...

She couldn't allow herself to dwell on the wishing part. She had other important things to take care of, and this time, she really had something to fix. The sense of longing remained.

Regardless, they were going home tomorrow, she thought as she put the hood of her coat over her head, going back to their lives. Their friendship. Certain subjects, they might never raise again. That, too, came with a sense of sadness.

# Chapter Twelve

## ANA

By the time Stevie returned, it was dark outside, Ana was halfway through the book and hungry. She could have gotten more of the truffles, maybe, but that was her gift to Stevie regardless of the current situation, and so she showed some restraint.

Her coat open, Stevie stood in the middle of the room, looking indecisive, a bit lost even.

Ana's heart went out to her, habit or simply expression of an emotion she couldn't deny, but she didn't think she could help her, not when she was still this overwhelmed, and terrified of her future outside the bubble of Angel Falls.

"Would you like to go and grab dinner?" Stevie asked.

"I thought you'd never ask." It would have been too easy, to go back to the way they'd always been, but that would mean pretending nothing ever happened. "I mean, yes. Just not the diner."

She was certain that whoever they'd run into, that person would be kind and understanding. Any more kindness of strangers, and it would break her.

"That's okay. How about we try the pizzeria Jo recommended?"

"I could go for pizza," she agreed.

"Okay. So...do you like it?"

It took Ana a moment to realize Stevie was talking about the book. "Oh yes, it's pretty good. I haven't yet figured out who the stalker is."

"It's an interesting premise—" Stevie took a deep breath. "But I'll shut up now, because I don't want to spoil you."

There are worse things to keep from someone, Ana almost replied, but she didn't want to be mean.

"Good." She got to her feet and picked up her coat. "Let's find that pizzeria, because I'm starving."

·•·♥·♥·♥·•·

They found the restaurant easily on a corner of Main Street, and to Ana's relief they didn't know any of the patrons. The owner came out to greet them and see them to a fairly private table.

A server brought their menus, and when he asked for their drink choices, Ana went for a Chianti.

"Same for me," Stevie said. "Thank you."

"Wait, please...We'll have the bottle instead."

Stevie's eyebrows shot up to her hairline.

"What? It's our last night in Angel Falls, and we won't have to check out until noon. You don't think I can handle my liquor?"

Stevie's gaze dropped to the tablecloth, and she picked up her napkin and unfolded it.

"I wasn't thinking that. I know you can handle anything."

"Please, don't start."

"I won't. Let me just say, I hope you can forgive me someday. I only meant to help...but I know, I understand, I shouldn't have done that. I know you never needed me to."

"Stevie."

"Okay. Sorry."

Ana went back to studying her food options, wondering what the right time would be, the right way. Seeing her friend suffer didn't bring her any relief. She couldn't just let it go either, and she knew that sooner or later, they would have to have that conversation. But not now. She glanced at her phone, but the radio silence continued.

Perhaps for the first time since the conflict had started, she was more angry than sad.

*They* were embarrassed by her, really?

Stevie's family, Patricia's, that of her lesbian colleague, Leyla and Jo, they were all proof that it wasn't all that hard, all that much to ask of someone to start from a point of kindness.

At least where this subject was concerned. Ana wasn't without fault, and she was aware of it, but this...

"You were right about them, I have to give you that," she said. When the server had filled their glasses, she picked up hers and raised it. "I still don't want to talk about it, but let's drink to Angel Falls. They might not make wishes comes true, but they are decent people."

"They are."

She did it a bit hesitantly, but Stevie clinked her glass against Ana's.

"To Angel Falls."

Things might never be completely the same, but some habits remained: They decided to choose different pizzas and share half of each. Other than the kindness of its residents, Ana would remember the amazing food they'd had in this town, from the breakfast at the inn, the various dishes Leyla and their staff served, the fancy Asian fusion restaurant she and Stevie had visited on the first night, hand-made truffles, and now yummy Italian food.

"This is so good," she couldn't hold back the comment. "I might take Leyla up on the job offer, so I can come back to eat in all those places."

Stevie answered her musings with a smile, a pensive and somewhat cautious air about her.

"Could you live in a place like this?" Ana asked. "Back in high school, I remember thinking that our town felt far too small, especially after my family had just moved there. We both wanted out of a place that must have been three, four times bigger than Angel Falls."

"Probably. But I think everyone wants out of the city where they went to high school, don't they?"

Ana had imagined she would, especially when her parents hadn't involved her in the decision to move at all. She had been resentful, but mostly scared to start over in a new school, with new classmates, leaving her friends behind. No, the truth was she had been more afraid they would easily leave her behind.

She had lost touch with those over the year, though her last year of high school had turned out to be so much better than expected because of Stevie. College, even better.

"I'm still mad at you, you know," she said, and took a sip of her wine.

"I know." Stevie held her gaze. "I'm so—"

She stopped when Ana waved her hand.

"I'm mad because I want to stop talking to you, and blame you for everything that went wrong, but then you gave me these great books, you offer me chocolates, and your taste in pizza is still as perfect as it has ever been..." She was aware she was rambling, but the wine was starting to melt down her inhibitions.

Sharing drinks and food with Stevie, and baring her soul, this was much needed familiarity.

"I'm glad you approve."

Stevie wasn't joking.

"I do. I do, even when I don't want to."

"It wasn't my place, to do, or to assume anything. I was so afraid you'd be disappointed if it didn't work out that I didn't realize I was way over the line—or that you were perfectly capable of assessing how realistic it would be."

"Right."

Again, Ana was struggling to find the words, and perhaps this was why she had wanted to postpone this conversation. Indefinitely, if possible.

"I know I'm not very good at this. I still had to do it my way."

How would she have reacted if Stevie had come to her one day and suggested a magic solution to a very realistic problem? Ana could give herself the answer. Their roles would never be reversed like this. She reflected on the day she had sprung the idea on Stevie, realizing she had probably given her reason to worry.

Not that it was an excuse.

But still.

"I didn't mean to ruin our friendship. Or Christmas."

She had made a mistake. But...

"Our friendship isn't ruined, and neither is Christmas," she declared firmly. "As for my family, you didn't break anything that wasn't already about to break...maybe helped speed up the process, even if you didn't mean to."

If they weren't in public, now might be the time for a good cry, for both of them, but the daunting realization wasn't going to stop her from enjoying a perfectly good pizza, and this bottle of Chianti.

She could be stubborn too.

95

"I need a little time, okay?"

"You got it," Stevie answered without hesitation.

*Have Yourself a Merry Little Christmas* was playing in the background, and for the first time since she had hung up with her mother, Ana had hope that she and Stevie could be back on the right track, maybe not today, or tomorrow, but soon.

Because Ana knew that losing Stevie would be so much worse than having to forgive her.

The tears came later that night when she was lying awake, thinking that ignorance had been bliss all this time when she refused to see how far her family's prejudice went. She was crying quietly so as not to wake Stevie but didn't succeed. Ana didn't mind so much when Stevie pulled her into a close embrace.

No words necessary.

# Chapter Thirteen

## STEVIE

S o much wine. At first it had been to overcome the awk-
wardness, then to celebrate the relief, and at the end of that
bottle, things almost felt normal between them.

That didn't mean they could turn back time.

There was no way for Ana to undo being confronted with
her family's ignorance.

No way for Stevie to undo her biggest mistake either.

She had half-feared Ana would push her away, but then she
didn't, and she just held her close, stroking her hair until they
both slipped into sleep.

The room was still dark when she woke. Stevie soon realized
that it wasn't because of the night sky, but a storm raging outside. That, and it was a lot later than she had thought, past 11:00
a.m. She stood at the window, her jaw dropping at the sight. Or
lack thereof. She couldn't even see past the inn's backyard. And
they would have to check out in about forty-five minutes.

"What is this?" Ana asked behind her, making her flinch.

"I don't know. A storm?"

"I can see that, but how...? They didn't say anything on the app."

It had been snowing all evening while they were at the restaurant, and later, when they had walked home. This, however, was different, heavy, persistent snowfall. She barely dared to say it out loud, but Ana beat her to it.

"Oh no. How will we get out of here now? Stevie!"

"Yes! I'm sure we'll figure something out." Not today, if the weather continued like that. "Let's get ready and have breakfast first, and then we regroup," she decided. "Maybe it will stop soon."

It didn't look that way, but Ana had already left in a huff, and moments later, Stevie could hear the sound of the shower. She wasn't sure she grasped Ana's state of mind correctly, not that there was any time to ponder this.

They still had to leave the room, and so, while Ana was in the bathroom, Stevie took the time to pack, haphazardly make the bed and move the many giftbags closer to the door, few of them the gifts they had given each other, most of them the ones Ana had bought to bring her family. It was doubtful now that she'd make it to family dinner, even if said family had expected and wanted her there.

Not sure what to expect, Stevie waited until Ana returned. Wearing only a towel. Stevie had a hard time averting her eyes. She could feel her face flush.

Ana gave the multitude of bags a long look and sighed. "I'll just take my gifts, I think. The rest...I don't know, we could leave them. Maybe someone could donate them."

"Are you sure?"

"Yes. No," she confessed. "You can go in. I'll just get dressed here." She let the towel fall to the floor.

When Stevie got in the shower, her cheeks were still burning.

No time, she reminded herself. Jo had been more than ac-commodating, but they didn't want to overstay their welcome. Time to go home and face the music.

⋅♥⋅♥⋅♥⋅♥⋅♥⋅

Unlike Ana, Stevie had brought her clothes with her, and after half-drying her hair, she packed up her toiletries as well and returned to their room, where Ana sat on the bed fully dressed, staring at her phone.

*No, wait*, Stevie's phone.

"Um, that is kind of private."

"You went on a dating app without telling me?" Ana ap-peared genuinely hurt by that.

Why?

"I'm sorry. You had a lot on your mind, and I thought it was time..."

Wait, why was she apologizing?

"And, is it? Did you find someone?" Now, that sounded almost aggressive. Ana's emotions were still all over the place, which wasn't a surprise, but Stevie found it increasingly more difficult to catch up with them.

She reached out to take the phone from her and sat beside her.

"Actually, I got a few messages, but I didn't have the time or inclination to look at any of them. We were a little busy, remember?"

"Yeah." Ana looked down at her hands. "I'm sorry. About everything. Dragging you here..."

"That's fine. You didn't have to try hard," Stevie tried to lighten the atmosphere, though, unbidden, her heart started to beat faster.

"True." Ana smiled wistfully. "For being so mean...and for stealing your phone. It's really none of my business." She turned to look at Stevie, holding her gaze. "Even if I want it to be."

It might be too early, it might be another mistake, but all Stevie could think of was how soft her lips looked, and how much she wanted to kiss her. She was tired of being worried and afraid. She leaned in carefully, and Ana met her halfway.

In another room, someone abruptly cranked up the radio, *It's the Most Wonderful Time of the Year* playing, a child squealing, but neither of them cared.

They both had waited too long for this moment. Both of them, Stevie realized, thrilled breathless when Ana kissed her back, cupping her face in her hands, her lips warm and soft as their kiss turned from sweet to suggestive, open to all possibilities.

"We have about five minutes to leave the room," Stevie whispered, her face warm under Ana's gentle hands. It wasn't like she had never touched her before, but not like this. With intent.

"I know. I don't want to." She sat back though, a soft smile playing over her beautiful features. "I was afraid all of this was only in my mind."

"It wasn't. I promise."

Stevie pulled her close for another kiss, then drew her into an embrace and held her tightly.

"I am so, so sorry, but I'll do better. I promise."

"You've been the best friend I could ask for, all these years. But maybe I'm asking for more."

Ana, who was always worried about not finding the right words, was expressing herself quite clearly.

"I think I'm more than fine with what you're asking for, but I suppose we'll have to get back to that later."

·♥·♥·♥·♥·♥·

Christmas magic and joyful revelations aside, the next few days wouldn't be easy. But they wouldn't be as terrible as Stevie had feared either. They still had conversations ahead, with each other. Likely, Ana and her family. But today was Christmas Eve, and finally being honest to each other, and themselves, was the best possible gift.

When they walked into the breakfast room, Ana's hand stole into hers, and that felt both familiar and excitingly new.

Jo came in a second later, greeting them with her usual cheery attitude.

"Good morning, you two. What weather for Christmas Eve, huh?"

"It sure is. We just came down here to grab a bite, but we did clear the room already."

"Oh, you didn't have to do that. No one's going anywhere in the next few hours, with what is coming down right now."

Stevie saw the flash of panic on Ana's face, determined to clear any potential misunderstanding right away.

"What do you mean?"

"We get these storms every now and then," Jo explained. "All the roads will be blocked, and it usually takes a day or so until everything is back to normal. No one can leave at the moment, so I suggest we wait it out, and if all else fails, I have everything for a Christmas Eve feast. Gifts too," she said with a smile. "Unless a miracle happens, we'll all be here until tomorrow."

Ana pulled a chair and sank into it.

"All right. I can't say I'm disappointed when there's nowhere else I need to be."

Stevie squeezed her hand gently. She sensed that Jo understood a whole lot more than she let on.

"Sit down, have breakfast first, please, and the room is yours as long as you need it."

"Thank you so much, but we'll pay for this night," Stevie told her. "Are you sure? The other guests..."

"Arrived last night, and we are fully booked now. We're not expecting anyone else at the moment, so it'll all work out. Don't worry. It will be okay. But you look like you could use some coffee."

"Oh yes," Ana sighed. "Please."

"Coming right up."

"Are you really okay with this?" Stevie asked when she had left.

On the table, she reached for Ana's hand again.

"Am I okay? Maybe not 100%, not yet," Ana admitted. "But I will be. And with this? These are some of the nicest people I've ever met in my life. Aside from you, of course. Spending Christmas Eve with you is the best turn of events I can imagine."

"I wish I had another gift for you, for tonight."

"You already gave me three." Ana's expression turned serious. "I'm not counting, and why would I? You've given me more than I could ever pay back." She straightened when there were voices coming from the hallway, and a moment later Jo returned with Leyla who stopped to say hello before the two of them sat down at another table.

"Like Jo said, it will be fine. More than fine. We'll be with people who want us here."

*I love you.* The thought was so intense Stevie was surprised she hadn't said it out loud. But she would, not long from now. The momentum had shifted again, and this time it was in their favor.

"I am so sorry. That should be your family."

"Yes, it should be, but I'm done making excuses for their shortcomings. I won't shut the door, but I'll take a break from trying so hard. And I want to be in the moment, here, with you."

102

"I want that too. But what about your wish?"

"It already came true," Ana said, looking so stunningly serene it made Stevie wonder what she had written on that paper. Perhaps, deep down, she already knew.

It was likely matching her own.

# Chapter Fourteen

## ANA

She could do this, be out here in the open, holding hands without the fear of being watched or judged, Ana thought as they sat in the breakfast room, feeling serene and joyful at the same time. She could kiss Stevie.

Perhaps not right now, but she could definitely do it again, and she wanted it so much. How was that for Christmas magic, and wishes coming true? She had been right after all, about Angel Falls, and the Wishing Tree, but most of all about finding her courage even if she couldn't always find the perfect words.

And it wasn't a surprise at all that it was with Stevie.

In the end, what she had written down on the paper was simple, perhaps vague, but specific enough for whatever Higher Power might be listening to hopeful people who entrusted their deepest desires to a tree.

*I want to be loved.*

When Stevie had picked her up at home at the beginning of their journey, Ana had full paragraphs on her mind. *Dear Mom* *and Dad, Harrison, Phoebe, Janelle, I wish you could see that I haven't changed. This is who I am, who I've always been, and there's nothing wrong...*She had rejected and raged against the lesson that was becoming clearer with each day, that she had done everything she could, that it was up to them now...but there was something Ana still could do, be with people who accepted her, who didn't blink an eye.

I want to be loved.

In the end, it had been easy as soon as she stopped banging her head against the wall.

It might not have been what she had imagined at first, but it was slowly starting to heal the wounds which were the reason why she had come here.

·♥·♥·♥·♥·♥·

The snow hadn't let up when they went back to their room, and as minutes, then an hour, passed by, Ana could sense her initial stress reaction melting away. She sent a text to her parents to let them know she wouldn't make it, regardless of whether she was invited or not. She kept the last part to herself.

Ana caught Stevie casting a thoughtful glance at the many packages. She got up and joined her, thrilled when Stevie put her arms around her. She had always been comfortable around her, seeking her closeness, but this was different, in an exciting way. Stevie had no idea how exciting.

"I thought I might leave them for people to donate, but now that we have a Christmas party to attend...You were right, I went way over the top." *Can't buy me love*, she thought, the tinge of sadness fleeting. "Anyway, I thought I might bring a few of them downstairs. And I'll send the others to my family. If they get them a few days later, that doesn't take away the meaning, does it?"

"No, definitely not," Stevie agreed.

"In fact, I could wrap them right now, and we can drop them off at the post office tomorrow. I'll ask Jo if she has something I can use."

"Sure. I could go..."

"I'm coming with you," Ana declared, and Stevie's smile was more than worth it. She had so many things still to tell her. She knew she'd struggle at times, but somehow the realization didn't bother her so much anymore. She knew Stevie would be patient. With everything.

"Okay, let's see if Jo can find us something." They brought some of the gifts down to the decorated breakfast room that would be the location for the dinner party later, then sought out their host at the counter.

As they'd hoped, Jo was helpful. She laughed at their inquiry. "My friends, here in Angel Falls we never run out of wrapping paper or packing materials. Come with me, take a look, and take what you need."

She led them to a storage room in the back, where one entire corner was indeed dedicated to packages, paper and tapes.

"Wow. This is..."

"Amazing," Stevie finished for her.

"If you have a reputation for being dedicated to Christmas, everything needs to be in place all the time," Jo commented. "Excuse me," she added when they could hear voices from the reception area. "I have to go check if they need anything. Just pull the door closed behind you when you're done."

"Thank you so much!" Ana called after her, and then they were alone. She placed a quick kiss on Stevie's lips because she could and chose a few items.

"What was that for?"

"Oh, you know. It's Christmas and I'm in love with my best friend. Against all odds, and I might remind you that there were plenty of odds...I'm happy."

"Me too," Stevie admitted, and then, they were kissing again, and it was everything Ana had ever hoped for from that first moment of realization. It all made sense now that though she had liked Patricia, she never fully connected with her.

Even her anger at Stevie for trying to fix something Ana had known deep down wasn't in their hands. Maybe she had always known that it would come to this, and she would have to make a choice. Stevie had shown her long before the people of Angel Falls that kindness was a choice, and that love didn't come with conditions.

"I'm so sorry to interrupt, but could you come join us for a moment?"

Ana stepped back, blushing, but Jo didn't mind their semi-public display of affection. She and Stevie picked up the packaging materials and went back outside, where Ana stopped cold when she saw the people standing at the reception counter.

"Auntie Ana!" Her nephew let go of his mother's hand, and ran to her, hugging her hard. Her legs, mostly, so she crouched down to give him a proper hug.

"Cory! How come you are here?" She squeezed one more time and got up. "How come you are all here?" She had to be dreaming. It wasn't possible that her aunt Carolyn, her cousin Gia, her sister-in-law Janelle and Cory had all come to the Christmas Inn. Hope flared briefly, but she quickly realized that her entire family hadn't come to the same conclusions.

She watched as Cory smiled at Stevie, and it came to her once more that she had always been family.

"Well, I hoped we'd see you tonight at your parents' dinner, but after I talked to your father, I realized that wasn't the case," Carolyn revealed. "Even though it's Christmas, I gave him a piece of my mind, something I should have done a long time ago, and so, Gia and I packed up things to come here. We arrived yesterday evening, just before the storm."

"Same here," Janelle said. "I didn't tell anyone except Harrison. He wasn't too happy, but he understands, and we thought you shouldn't be alone on Christmas."

"I'm not, but...That's kind of you. Thank you."

"Well, that, and after I read about the Wishing Tree, and the Christmas Inn, I couldn't resist. This is a beautiful place."

Jo beamed with pride.

"It is. You've met Jo. You all know Stevie."

"Of course," Gia and Janelle said in perfect unison, before Ana interrupted them.

"My girlfriend."

Stevie cast her a quick surprised smile that Ana caught through a somewhat blurry vision. She couldn't believe this was happening, Christmas in this magical place, with Stevie, new-found family and people in her original one who cared more than she had dared to hope.

"It's so great you're all here. I can give you your gifts in person, and...It means a lot to me."

Immediately, she was folded into more hugs.

They sat down in the breakfast room, and Jo provided all of them with coffee, hot chocolate and more of her famous cookies while they caught up.

Cory had decided that Stevie's lap was the place where he wanted to be, and not long after, he fell asleep. Ana couldn't stop smiling, even though her happiness was laced with melancholy. One day, maybe, her parents would see and understand just how much love she had to give, how much joy was possible for her, for them. But if they didn't, she couldn't let it hold her back from living her life, with the person who was always meant to be in it.

She had always had family. Christmas. And love. She was going to celebrate all of it every day of her life.

Jo and Leyla joined them later, and Ana couldn't help thinking out loud.

"How many rooms does this inn have anyway? Do they magically increase?"

"That part isn't magic," Jo admitted, laughing. "We always keep a certain number of rooms for family, and for stories that take a different turn due to Christmas magic. Basically, all our guests are family, but you know what I mean."

Ana did. She followed Jo's gaze to the window, realizing the snow had stopped, rays of sun making their way through the clouds.

Jo got to her feet. "All right, time to get out there and make at least a bit of a path."

Ana took a look around the table, her gaze resting on Stevie who nodded.

"How many shovels do you have?"

# Chapter Fifteen

## STEVIE

A little faith could make a big difference. Or reason, even. It had never been her job to convince anyone. A part of Ana's family had found their way to Angel Falls all on their own. It mattered.

They spent most of the afternoon playing in the snow and clearing enough of it away so Jo and her staff had a path to the street.

Little Cory had a blast building a snowman with her and Leyla, as Ana and Gia were chatting, beyond excited.

Stevie stopped for a moment to watch her.

Ana.

Her girlfriend.

Regardless of the outside temperature, the thought warmed her, with all the hope and possibilities life had put in their way.

Or, more likely, they had always been there—she and Ana had chosen to open their eyes to them.

Because of the name of the town, it was impossible not to make snow angels, wasn't it?

No one asked them any intrusive questions, no one judged.

This was the Christmas she wanted to give to Ana, though she had written a different wish on the paper.

That tree was magic after all.

"Okay, thank you so much everyone!" Slightly self-conscious, Jo added, "I want to point out that we still don't make it a habit to make guests work, but I'm so grateful you all did. Now, get inside and out of those wet clothes, and we'll continue all warm and cozy later in the breakfast room. Remember, formal wear."

"Really?" Stevie wondered out loud. "I'm not sure we brought..."

"No, of course not. There's only one rule. Be comfortable and merry. Be you. Oh wait, that's three, but I think you can all handle it. I'll see you later."

Stevie had to admit there was something awe-inspiring about the excitement of Christmas Eve, as long as all the stars aligned. But even almost perfect was beyond amazing.

·♥·♥·♥·♥·♥·

Even though dressing up was not a requirement, she was happy to, combining black pants with a shiny top and the necklace Ana had given her four Christmases ago—the small Christmas tree pendant seemed like a premonition now.

Ana returned from the bathroom wearing a red dress and stockings, stopping in the middle of the room. Stevie was trying not to stare, but apparently, she hadn't been successful.

"Too much?" Ana asked. "I know what Jo said, but..."

"Gorgeous," Stevie told her. "I feel underdressed."

"No way. You are..." A soft blush colored her cheeks. "You are amazing."

112

"Thank you. I still messed up, and I'm aware. I promise, I'll never do anything like that..."

Ana put a finger to her lips.

"I know."

Sharing another kiss felt so natural, and inevitable. Her hands went from Ana's back to her waist, and she pulled her closer. Sure, they didn't have a lot of time, and voices in the hallway were a clear indication that some guests were already on their way down, but who cared?

They made a few steps towards the bed, before Ana pulled back and sat. Stevie wasn't entirely sure how to interpret her expression, so she went with the obvious.

"I'm sorry. I know this is not the time, and I don't want to make you go downstairs in wrinkly clothes..."

"The clothes are fine," Ana assured her with a soft smile. She reached out a hand, and Stevie took it and sat next to her.

"What's the matter?"

"You know, there was a reason why Patricia and I broke up that had nothing to do with my parents, or me not coming out enough. She didn't like that you were always around, and she could get very insecure about it." Ana paused for a moment. Stevie waited.

"Anyway, I got annoyed about it sometimes, but maybe I owe her an apology. She was right about something. I couldn't really commit, and the truth is, I didn't want to. Not when I knew it would never feel the same."

At this point, Stevie held her breath, starting to feel a bit lightheaded, until Ana said, "It's always been you," and she could finally exhale.

"I know what you mean."

·♥·♥·♥·♥·♥·

The evening passed in a blur, yet it would forever remain vivid in Stevie's memory, food and drink, gifts, the company. Stevie had opened a video chat with her mother, Evan, and his new girlfriend Catherine waving in the background.

"I can't wait to meet you and Ana," she said.

"Same here." Ana was standing beside her.

"Then I have an idea," Stevie's mom said. "Why don't we all go visit Stevie this year for Christmas?"

Yes, why not?

*Wait—*

Her panic must have shown on her face because Evan added, "Or we can come over a few days later. No problem."

"No, that's fine," Ana assured him. "We'll leave here early tomorrow, and that gives us plenty of time. We got it covered."

Plenty of time might have been an exaggeration, but if Ana was certain, Stevie could be too.

"Yes, we do. See you tomorrow."

There was always room for more joy, Christmas or any day.

·♥·♥·♥·♥·♥·

Before they left the next morning, Leyla handed them a small square package, about 6x6 inches.

"We have one last gift for you. And we hope to see you back here someday. Ana, the job offer still stands."

"Thank you, but I think I have to pass on that for now. But we'd love to return sometime in the future. Can we open it now?"

"Please do."

Stevie, with her mind full of beautiful scenarios of the future, watched as Ana opened the gift, revealing a Christmas ornament in the shape of a tree.

Not just any tree.

"I hope this will remind you that you can find family anywhere, even when you least expect it." With a smile, they added, "And that Christmas magic exists."

"Oh, I know," Stevie returned. "Thank you so much. It's been wonderful meeting all of you."

"Same here. Merry Christmas."

"Merry Christmas, and a safe trip home."

It occurred to Stevie that no one seemed to doubt that from now on, she and Ana would have one Christmas tree together. When her gaze met Ana's, she realized that the two of them knew it too.

"The merriest," Ana whispered.

# *Epilogue*

## ANA

With the streets finally cleared, they made it to the post office to mail her packages and go home from there. She had exchanged polite Merry Christmas messages with her parents and siblings, and left it at that, feeling grateful and serene, no lack of Christmas spirit.

And it wasn't even over yet.

Their ride home was quiet and relaxed, music playing. She drove, focusing on the road, which was such an adequate metaphor for the rest of her life. After being too timid, too worried about what others might think, she was back in the driver's seat.

A wish come true. Christmas magic. Her own doing. At a red light, she cast a look at Stevie.

"How do you feel about Christmas now?"

Stevie smiled.

"I'll have to tell Mom I'm sorry, but I'm loving it, dates and rituals and all of it. Somehow, I don't think she'll mind."

"No. She, and your dad too, they just wanted you to be happy."

Ana was a bit surprised she could state this without sadness, but she'd been around Stevie's family enough to know it was simply a fact. Janelle thought that Harrison and Phoebe would come around, and that they would bring their parents along. Ana hadn't given up hope entirely, but she wasn't going to sit around waiting either.

After all, they had a Christmas party to plan.

"Wait, do you even have a tree at home?" she asked, and Stevie gave her a blank stare. "Um...I didn't really expect anyone to visit me, so...no?"

"Don't worry," Ana said, leaning back into her seat with a smile. "Just let me take care of everything."

When they stopped at a diner for a coffee and snack, she laid out her plan.

Her turn to pull off a miracle, even though Stevie's mom and brother might not expect it. In fact, they had no idea what they had gotten themselves into.

"Do you trust me?" she asked.

"I do," Stevie answered without hesitation, and to Ana, it was a sign of beautiful things to come.

# STEVIE

She had met a couple of Evan's girlfriends, but she'd never seen him completely and utterly smitten.

"Look who's talking," he returned when she whispered it to him, and he couldn't have been more right.

The occasion was bittersweet, as she was certain how much her father would have loved this. They were flexible where it counted, he'd always said. Dates and rituals were negotiable, respect, kindness, and love weren't.

*I hear you.*

He would have loved Angel Falls too. Stevie might not be able to talk to him, but this year, more than ever, she could feel his presence, and that was some kind of magic too.

Ana had pulled off the impossible, and so the five of them were having a Christmas feast, with dishes they had cooked, and partly bought prepared, thanks to *Groceries around the World* that was open when most other businesses weren't. The result was both traditional and wildly eclectic. Both her mother and Catherine had traveled extensively, more than anyone else at the table, and they were excited to share stories about their adventures, and similar food they had tried.

Ana had also brought her entire decorated tree from her apartment in a cab, back in time to help Stevie with dinner, and make a batch of cookies which she finished decorating minutes before the doorbell rang.

The champagne they had bought was local, the wine for dinner from Argentina, appetizers Mediterranean, and the main course Eastern European, the dessert Japanese, and somehow it was perfect.

"I felt a bit bad for inviting ourselves, but I can't anymore. This is wonderful," Mom said, casting a smile at the lit tree. It had made the journey without problem, only a few strands of tinsel had stayed behind in the cab, and they had to rearrange the lights.

"I have only one question left."

"Another piece of cake? Coffee? Or a nightcap?" Stevie offered.

"No, I'm good. But since you're all here, and I'm so happy and excited you are...Who's going to give me grandchildren first?"

"Mooom," Stevie and Evan protested in perfect unison, while Catherine blushed, and Ana smiled widely.

Stevie couldn't take her eyes off her. Yes, because she was beautiful, and Stevie could finally admit to herself that she looked at her that way.

She couldn't help noticing the amazing change that had taken place. There was a new confidence about Ana, a determination that made her even more irresistible. Stevie couldn't deny it, she was head over heels for her, thrilled to discover what the future held for them. And her protest aside, there was no one else she could have ever imagined starting a family with.

There was no one but Ana for her.

"What? You both made excellent choices. Evan, you kept Catherine to yourself for far too long. And Ana, aside from the fact that you're a gifted cookie decorator...you've been family since the day Stevie came home from school and couldn't stop talking about you."

Ana laughed, even though her eyes were welling up.

"I'm sure I did the same that day. Thank you, and Merry Christmas."

"Merry Christmas, Ana."

Everyone raised their glasses and exchanged wishes, before Ana got to her feet.

"There's just one more thing missing. I am so grateful to be here with all of you. Stevie...Especially you. Would you do this with me?"

Stevie joined her at the tree, where they hung the ornament Leyla had gifted them, a symbol of many more magical Christmases to come.

They kissed to applause that was a much louder sound than three people should be able to make.

Stevie thought she must have been really good this year, because every single item on her Christmas list had come true.

# About the Author

B arbara Winkes writes sapphic crime drama and Christmas romance. She loves writing characters who get the job done, whether it's stopping a predator or saving cherished traditions—while still making time for love. She lives with her wife in Quebec City.

barbarawinkes.com

# Also by Barbara Winkes

*Bells Will Be Ringing*
*A Girlfriend for Christmas*
*Christmas Cupid*
*Destination Christmas, Next Stop Love*
*The Christmas Memory*

Printed in Great Britain
by Amazon

49653156R00078